DonQuell Speller

AF072906

I, Dee Claire War Too!

by
DonQuell Speller

The Betrayal Edition

Lavish Life 88 Entertainment
Charlotte, NC

☙1❧

I, Dee Claire War Too!

Copyright © 2015 by DonQuell Speller

Softcover 978-1-943079-22-3
eBook: 978-1-943079-23-0

All rights reserved. No parts of this book may be reproduced or transmitted in any form or by any means, electronic or mechanical, including photocopying, recording, or by any information storage and retrieval system, without permission in writing from the publisher or authors.

Darnell Jacobs
DonQuell Speller

This is a work of fiction. Names, characters, places and incidents either are the product of the author's imagination or are used fictitiously, and any resemblance to any actual persons, living or dead, events, or locales is entirely coincidental.

Any people depicted in stock imagery provided by Thinkstock are models, and such images are being used for illustrative purposes only. Certain stock imagery provided by © Thinkstock.

This book was printed in the United States of America.

Acknowledgments

This is a fictitious book. I, the writer and the publisher, also do not support any violence, criminal activity, promotion of drug distribution, or usage. We strongly condemn any disrespect towards all local, state and federal government, and fully support our brave soldiers and troops who fight every day to keep our freedom alive.

Those in law enforcement who serve and protect us, the law and discrimination isn't the form of justice, we thank you for your dedication and hard work.

My sincere thanks goes to, Shawn L. Jennings for lacing me with the hot poetic verses which are always on time. I truly admire your work and wish you much success in the near future. "What is Betrayal?"

Special thanks to Romids "Ro" Miles, his beautiful mother, Tina Miles Holder, brother, and sister, Tekia Thomas. Ro takes the time to read every book I write and keeps it real if I'm slacking and need to go in harder.

I dedicate this book to Rhoda Wilkins, Linda Hall, Beverly Gainy and the Gainy sisters, Ivene Robinson, Sabrina Poe, Lisa Leak, Barbara McCoy, Lisa Bridges, all the real women who've always had my back and still do.

The Betrayal

There's not a single soul living or dead who hasn't betrayed or fell victim to it or both. And sadly, as much as we encounter it, we never get used to it, it's here until the end since it started from the beginning.

DonQuell R. Speller.

What is Betrayal?

Is betrayal a constant reminder that giving a person too much credit, too early a consistent, yet an almost unavoidable attribute that makes us human?

Betrayal is more hurtful when unexpected. But it almost begs the question; did we invigorate a person's envy or jealousy? Because of their own insecurities not taken into consideration by us, who they once felt shared a certain ligature of trust? Did we somehow subconsciously affront their iniquities which could have easily caused their invidious nature? When all the while our benign hearts omitted one's feelings through capricious behaviors that later caused betrayal, distrust which are foibles gone undetected, long enough to faster into common perils.

In some cases the enemy isn't the one who betrayed you, but rather the cantankerous person you've become by decimation of a strong friendship that eventually veered towards chaos. A self-inflicted wound, instead, it seems we have betrayed ourselves.

Betrayal, the frail enemy revealed, the carousel of lies and deceit, the image of the world burning, and the smell of lighter fluid on the ones you loved hands.

Damn, should've known better than to build trust out of paper love. The love for paper made you hate me more. Or did you really hate me before?

Betrayal, a controlled destruction of hell where people fall by the hands they never once began to cleanse, enemies you called friends, the future you thought was the past, the storm you sought to outlast, but your own foolishness become a nuisance to those you abeyant perpetuated. The one's you galvanized. So it's true.

The real enemy is you…

People have heard some of the old sayings on relationships that are somewhere along the lines of being very careful on how you acquire that special someone in your life. Because it just might be the same way that you lose them.

Most of us quite often betray our own beliefs by indulging in unidentified endeavors that go against the fabrics of our so-called morals and stringent values. And if true, the infidelity lies within thy self.

Compatibility wasn't put on the table almost as if compelled to be immediately dismissed, totally out of fear that the relationship would not work, which in return creates a façade. We then live in a state of temporary happiness until exposed then we point the fingers at those who we indiscriminately chose.

Betrayal taught me to never invest my all.

Because some take loans out on other people's hearts, and when they can't make the payments, they eventually foreclose certain strongholds that can cause minor strokes.

Despair creates depression which bleeds stress upon this nation you might find indignation having persuasion towards on illegal husbands, or promiscuous concubines. Whoever betrayed you became you.

An evolution of mind-pollution causes confession.

If only you could feed your mind a meta-mucil, you could get rid of the shit you're not used to.

Some people sacrifice their futures for things that ain't lucid. Then look to you when they seeking their retribution.

To ridicule, is to betray an individual.

It's pitiful that to some, it's considered criminal.

Previously.....

The Queen's City streets had a serious threat against them once the unbreakable codes of the streets began to get lost to the snitches. These were the types of snitches who would do anything, at all cost, to continue their lifestyles; even if it forced them to live on the run in shame, or caused the demise of their lives or even the lives of their love ones.

The notorious drug dealer, A.K.A "Whack" finds himself in the clutches of the law and given an ultimatum by the D.E.A. to hand over his best friend and crime partner, Jamal "J-Mack" Raqib, or never leave the gloomy prison cell of the Federal Institution they planned to bury him in. Whack chose the latter, thus handing Jamal on a silver platter.

Jamal is arrested for murder and a slew of other criminal charges, and his life is all but over. With no one to turn to, he sends word to his brother in South Bronx, who then drives to Charlotte with two things on his mind; win his brother's freedom, and make those who had him incarcerated pay.

Unfortunately, Whack is found out and before he goes into hiding, the two ruthless killers clash, leaving a string of bodies of so-called pawns and corrupted officials for the government to clean up.

Sulaiman finds the love of his life. She was a single white rose in a patch of thorns, who happened to be a Bronx native visiting her best friend. The two marry, shaking up a cartel tradition and infuriating folks who now want her blood.

A secret she's hidden from her husband was revealed after returning from the whirlwind honeymoon. Agents from out of nowhere converged upon her, leaving a distressed Sulaiman to search for answers.

The head of the Cartel is what he found his wife to be. But, of course, the highest ranking cartel member couldn't just walk away thinking it was over. Many said her days were numbered, a short life expectancy. Yet, there had been hits placed on her, but no one had the balls to carry out the orders, and those who had tried found themselves on the receiving end of the barrel.

Although, she swore to a lifetime of secrecy, one couldn't possibly think they could just simply quit and become a housewife overnight. Naw, the sudden change would bring about suspicion in the drug game, and suspicion in her profession brings about certain death. So, what began as minor nuances turned into a major pain in the ass, and again, she's forced to 'clean-up'.

This starts with 'tidying up the house'. The hunt for her mother's killers goes underway and her heart shows no vital signs when contemplating, yet, more deaths. And to Dee Claire War, as the streets call her, vengeance tastes sweeter than two male lovers dipped in a pool of pure honey. But first, she has to be released from her confinement to prick those who dare to ruin her happiness.

Prologue....

"Let it be death, but not humiliation. Let it be little, but not through others. He, who does not get by while sitting, will not get by standing either. The world has two days, one for you and the other against you. When the day is for you, do not feel proud, but when it is against you, endure it." She quoted the saying repeatedly, while consciously working the tasbeeh (Rosary) in her right hand, as she sat Indian style rocking rhythmically.

Zohra stood up. Again, she went pacing back and forth throughout the small cramped prison cell, trying to memorize her fortieth hadith, from the book her husband had sent three months ago. This morning she woke up at 4:32, *lotto numbers*…she'd thought to herself had she still been a kafir in the streets. Now, as she peered at her watch which read 5:43, it was minutes short of Subhe Saadiq 'true dawn'. It was early, too early to be up at four, especially when salat came in at 6:06 a.m. but today was her day.

Who would have thought, in a little less than five-hours, she'd be free, as free as the butterflies that greeted the flowers she'd placed outside of her windowsill, a beautiful scene indeed.

The window gazing was like watching her very own personal TV; it kept her away from the many negative vibes that went on all around her daily, and it most definitely kept her mind away from the many family and friends she'd lost in such a short period of time.

Sadly, back to back incidents kept her wondering what would happen next. Six months prior, she'd received word that her father sucked on the barrel of a .44 mag. Her uncle, also a policeman, had been in the kitchen when he'd heard the gun go off. Six weeks afterwards, her brother had written a letter to the federal prosecutors in the cowardly act of snitching. He'd made a deal for complete immunity of all charges in return for his complete cooperation. His devious intentions were to take over the throne in which he felt should have gone to him to begin with. He felt it was her fault that their parents were deceased. For all he cared, she could rot in prison for the rest of her betraying life. At one time, he loved his sister dearly, but he loved power and freedom more.

Victorious, as well as the other men in the cartel, were beyond furious with the decision allowing her to lead. Unbeknownst to them all, she was a bona fide survivalist taught by her uncle in the thick woods, forests and mountains of North Carolina, trained in weaponry.

She had been left for two days in the mountains of Asheville, N.C., where she slept on the ground, plodded through dense vegetation and foliage, braving the harsh conditions of the one hundred plus summer degrees, thus repeating the same training in the blizzard, snowy, craggy where she had to fend off the same hungry animals of the wild.

Her uncle, and another unknown, had drilled her relentlessly. The position she now held had been rightfully earned, by no means, given. A series of tests had proved that; the blisters on her feet at the age of 10, grappling in the flatlands wearing terrain boots in the

Middle East desert, and night-vision goggles at 15. Her first kill would determine if she'd fold mentally or physically, while encumbered by the weight of the dead woman chopped to small pieces in the duffle bag she carried. Dee Claire War hadn't asked a single question nor mentioned the kill to anyone, not even the mother she worshipped…..a mother who knew her daughter's every move.

Her brother Victorious' lackadaisical actions, and his quick temper, along with the drug habit he referred to as recreational had hindered his succession. Deep down inside, his jealousy ate at him for the favoritism shown to his *'can't-do-no-wrong'* sister, a sister who in fact had saved his ass many times.

Now, thanks to a jailor who was seeking a spot on the roster and money due to greed, a hand written letter from her brother in route to the federal D.A.'s office has been intercepted. The jailor had heard through the grapevine about her position. Although, the men were separated from the females, he knew a trusted trustee who worked on the bottom floor. The trustee would deliver the letter by way of folding it, and placing it in between her cold-cut sandwich, on her lunch tray. The jailor made sure to drill him and his buddy, making them aware of the importance of ensuring the contents arrived at its proper destination. The scheme alone was major, and if intercepted, the two would be facing felonies that would have them old men by the time they were released. The trustee awaited his payment, and once it arrived, she was given the correct tray during chow call.

Zohra took the top off of the sandwich. Before biting into it, she inspected her food before consuming it, something she'd been taught to do long ago. To her surprise, there was a folded sheet of paper sealed with clear scotch-tape. The letter had been stuffed inside of the sandwich, along with a personal letter from the source.

But that was months ago, now her blue eyes stared into the mirror, a trance deep enough to drown in 'Nostalgia' crept in while she refused to inhale the bitter taste of apprehension. Her mind began to indulge on the 'finer' days, when she'd met the most beautiful Black man her eyes had ever seen.

At first, she was reluctant to tell him the truth. The truth he'd found out by being surrounded by F.B.I. agents at LAX airport, embarrassingly in front of hundreds of by-standers and folks waiting on flights to come or go. At one point of time, she'd sat at the head seat to one of the world's most ruthless cartels. There were many to name and contend with who were up and coming. She had been responsible for ordering numerous hits on adversaries, and on some occasions, even their relatives. But only after meeting this new found love, did her world change.

Chapter One

In a whirlwind romance, Zohra as she now called herself, Dee Claire War, forever to the drug lords, had married the man of her dreams. But tangled in a web of deceit, she also had to deal with the changing of her faith and the racism that came along with being married to a Black man. She was facing an angry organization of criminals in which she'd turned her back on.

Sulaiman assured her that once the feds released her, a normal life awaited them both, something she seriously doubted, but nevertheless hoped for. One could run towards the future but couldn't escape the past, and all of her adult life she'd been running with scissors. Neither would ever see normal again.

Her husband struggled for months trying to find answers to questions she was unable to answer due to her unfortunate situation. Circumstances permitted the communication needed for true understanding, and those in her organization refused to provide him with any information relating to her, or the case. Well aware of the feds listening and watching their every move, even if she wanted to, she couldn't leave him or any of the others in charge, especially knowing they were eavesdropping on her phone conversations. Her businesses were under surveillance, electronic bugging devices had been planted in her cell, and there was a line of informants and other witnesses who had been subpoenaed to court to give testimonies. And, she was one-hundred percent sure they were eyeing him as well.

Sulaiman hated being lied to, but fully understood her plight, especially after dealing with her brother's circumstances. It was easy to be put into something and extremely difficult to find your way out. He also knew the importance of silence, which spoke volumes. He trusted him, even if it seemed ironic at the time, the *Boss*.....those four letter words meant he needed patience. The look in his eyes the day of her arrest showed that not in a million years, would he have thought of his wife running a multi-million dollar a week empire, making her one of the U.S. most sought-after drug traffickers and gun smugglers.

Dee Claire War loved him intensely. He was her only known weakness and it pained her to see him in such a state as the two U.S. Marshals who flanked her had her chained at the ankles and waist, and handcuffed like an animal. But, looks could be deceiving, and hers surely had him. With her training, she could've easily eluded arrest, but she thought about their marriage and the long term consequences.

For two decades, her mother had called the shots to the lucrative heroin and coke business, while everyone thought it was the father, including her brother. Until one day a family meeting had been called. All who were there had been shocked with the news which rocked the small Italian community. Jealousy and rage, both, caused their empire to be cowardly attacked from within the ranks.

Detectives and investigators had all failed miserably at their futile attempts. She kept her mouth closed, even with threats of life imprisonment and failed attempts to connect her to the killings of several informants. An unknown source delivered a list to him, and with the lists of names and locations, he returned the favor for helping him with Jamal, and cleaned-up everyone's sloppy mess. He'd racked up a staggering body count throughout the East Coast and beyond. All of this with limited contact, so as to not add to her list of burdens.

The more Sulaiman dug, the more complicated he understood his wife's life to be and wondered if she'd ever be free. At times, the weight of her imprisonment put a serious strain on their marriage. Suliaman was so busy handling the mess her people had created they barely had time for one another. She received mail on the fly, and she didn't get to see her babies.

Paris still remained, taking care of the mansion, notifying her of all the minor and major changes, and additions to the house. Nothing stopped for her. Things went on, the babies grew fast and pictures were a constant reminder of her role as mother and wife. Yet, all she was familiar with was the closing and opening of security doors, pat downs, and being surrounded by the living dead.

Dee Clair War had to learn to adjust. All of her life she'd been raised to give the orders, demanding a quick and professional response, but man, how things had changed, especially since she was literally on the other side of the fence. She wasn't used to being told when to get up, go to sleep, where to stand, sit, times to wash, eat etc… But, she refused to accustom herself to the dreadful prison life like so many countless others before her.

Unlike her fellow inmates, she thrusted herself head first into studying her case, the satiation of law book and other religious articles. Day-by-day, she found herself engrossed in knowledge, separating herself from those who took life unserious, not wanting to be with any particular groups, or person(s).

Prison had definitely become a warehouse for the criminally insane, a place where gangs ran rampant. There were females coming off of heroin and crack addictions, reliance of pain killers. This was a place where fights broke out over minute things, such as the T.V. and board games. Arguments would start over unintelligent debates and some of the dumbest conversations she'd ever heard. A good example would be: *which rapper has the biggest cock or which female artist has a fake ass.* But not Zohra, she had no time for the buffoonery. She sat back and observed, soaking up the different attitudes, learning to duplicate the swaggers of both coasts and all cultures, never knowing when she may need its usage.

Sulaiman advised her to sever ties with her cartel until she could get a full grasp of the treachery. It was a dysphoria decision, but there was just too much resentment and blood shed of family against family. People weren't following her orders and no one lived up to their word or bond, so enough with the disappointments. Far too much had taken place, ruining the business her family had built throughout the years. The combination of the different turmoil had caused one of the greatest power struggles ever witnessed on the East Coast.

Heeding the advice given by her husband, Dee Claire War proceeded with the dismantling of the cartel, infuriating numerous people who were directly targeted financially. The loss of jobs, power, and statuses agitated several key members on the committee who agonized over the blind-sided decision. With mouths to feed, expensive house mortgages, a life of luxury and a mixture of other important related issues, such as health care for the elderly, college tuition and private schools to name just a few, behind closed doors meetings were being held on taking strict and effective steps to rectify those current problems. A secret group separate from the committee was designed to handle the immediate situation, and from that point on the conspiring began.

After completing the daily ibaadat *"devotion"* she sat still, thinking about what she'd do first, once her feet touched the concrete. Would she make love to her husband, spend time with her adorable kids or put her culinary school skills to use and cook her very first family dinner? Actually, the plans were to do all of the above, she just hadn't figured out in which order. Also, high on her to-do list was to visit her parent's grave sites, and maybe her brother's, she was still undecided about that one.

Three funerals in such a short span of time, and she was unable to attend. Not being there had almost broken her spirit and it was a wonder Sulaiman stuck around. He'd been so understanding, caring, and definitely patience. The deceitful lies and ruined trust made it unbelievable he'd stayed through it all, and she would be forever grateful. No one had seen her brother's betrayal or greed; it blindsided them all.

Dreams of her brother's murder haunted her nightly. An intricate hit had poisoned not only him, but the trustees and a jailer as well. Officials who investigated the poison had confirmed by lab reports that they'd all eaten from the same exact food source. Dee Claire War's brother's face would appear late night, first in the ghostly form of complete darkness, then out of the blackness, a walking dead image which wailed and groaned. A full body came into view, walking zombie-like as it called out, *"Dee, why did you kill me?"* The annoying voice echoed hauntingly. But in reality, he knew perfectly well the reason for his own demise, just as the countless others did.

They had broken the code, the unforgivable rule of any streets, snitching. Their actions warranted stiff punishment, and it was bigger than wearing *'Stop Snitching'* tee-shirts and blasting someone's name on a Facebook page.

Not being able to attend her mother's funeral was by far one of the hardest things she'd ever had to endure, add to that the fact that she'd given birth to two beautiful babies in a federal detention center. To part with them had been extremely difficult mentally, but she knew they were in safe hands with Sulaiman and Paris. She owed Paris a debt she would never be able to repay.

Zohra requested Sulaiman not to bring the children to visit. She didn't want them to see her in such a predicament, regardless of how young the infants were. The visits were too emotionally draining. After each visit, once she'd returned to her cell block and entered her room, she'd cry her eyes out, only allowing God to see her flood gates open. Her newfound faith and prayers, along with the love of her husband and children is what kept her strong. The closer she'd get to the Lord, the more vulnerable she'd become.

At first, Zohra el Djemal felt as if she were somehow losing control. The more she pondered on the entire situation, the more she realized she'd never totally had a grip on things to begin with. Her current status and a mixture of the past drama sent tidewaters of emotions to hit the land of her fragile state. She had once prided herself as being a strong willed woman, unshakable and firm when it came to making some of life's toughest decision. Now, after so much death, the closer her steps came to regaining her freedom, the more she realized she'd be reentering into an unknown world with a faith half of the world unfairly grouped as radicals and extremists, or revenge from an opposing fraction, which made her more aware.

Zohra was more than grateful for the Lord protecting her and guiding her footsteps. At times, her unsteadiness had her wobbling in every direction the winds of sins blew in. Mobsters were sending their wives, girlfriends, or jump-offs to her, and each one would leave with a new addition to their face or belly, by a prison made shank. Things were serious on the inside, but luckily she never picked up a new set of charges.

The nightmares were just minutes away from being over. Just thinking about it warmed her icy heart. But, as long as the unburied bones which were piled sky high in the back of her filthy closet remained, she would never be able to totally submit herself to the Lord, nor those beneath Him.

Zohra skipped the morning breakfast. The anticipation of being with her loved ones wouldn't permit her to have an appetite. After giving the breakfast tray away, and a couple of items to the girls who had nothing, she completed the mingling and returned to her cell. Her belongings had already been packed the night before, since the Judge dismissed all of the charges against her, due to the lack of evidence and no witness to come forth. The D.A. had exhausted the opportunity to appeal, and that night, her attorney came to personally deliver the good news around 9:30 p.m. The appeal wasn't going to be pursued.

Zohra peered out of the window of her cell in deep thought. The sheer sound of keys jingling ripped her from the vivid day dream, "Dee Claire War!" A tall lanky guard yelled out, warning her of his approaching presence. "Pack up, it's time to go."

She hated that the guards wouldn't respect her name change to discontinue the use of Dee Claire War, and call her by Zohra el Dejmal, but she was sure they called her worst, terrorist and nigger lover to name a few.

The guard momentarily paused, allowing her to finish staring out of the window. He knew many contemplated their next move, but not Zohra. She marveled at the butterfly being wrapped gracefully by a determined spider. *What a sight,* she thought to herself, *nature or perhaps, a sign?* In that instant, she turned to grab her belongings and before she abandoned the cell for the next inmate to house, she took one last glimpse of the outside world, her next destination. She noticed the spider being devoured by a brown praying mantis, a little higher up in the food chain. The subliminal message sent a chill down her spine. *Has karma caught up with me?* She wondered as she exited the room.

Chapter Two

Zohra set her gaze upon the multi-culture of faces. Her eyes wandered throughout the small assembly of people who had gathered around, waiting on the release of their loved ones or friends.

With each step she took, her heart beat, erratically. She was anxious to leave, and in anticipation of seeing Sulaiman. But still, deep within the crevices of her cerebral cortex, a fear lingered. The expression on one's face could show various signs, signs that you feared no man, even if you were seconds away from shitting on yourself. Perhaps, even your practiced poker face, but in her line of work, the possibilities of your car exploding with the twist of a key, someone peeling your onion from a distance rooftop, a drive-by with a gunner or two on the back of a crotch-rocket riddling her body with bullets the width of a dime and length of a pencil, made one's limbs tremble a little.

With her eyes trained on her surroundings, she didn't see her husband nor did she see her attorney. *Maybe, I should question if I'm in the wrong area.* She thought, as she walked towards the front of the building. One particular tall beauty stood out clearly from the rest, immediately catching her eye; at first, it was the bright pink hijab almost exactly the same as hers, and the blue jeans a shade darker, but what shocked Zohra the most was, she was also wearing the same exact shoes as she was, which was extremely odd.

The two dressed head-to-toe, respectively, piqued Zohra's curiosity, especially since the female pushed a twin stroller and seemed to be coming in her direction with unwavering eyes trained on her. She was able to see the circumference of her face which was absolutely flawless, light-skinned complexion and a luminous smile. There in front of her lay a deadly viper depicted in the soul behind those eyes, a murderous gleam only a killer would notice, or someone at the end of a barrel.

"As Salaamu Alakum, Zohra." She gave the salutation, which automatically made Zohra focus on the babies. "King Sulaiman sent me to pick you up."

Zohra returned the greeting. "Why isn't he here?" she questioned on the verge of being upset, concern over shadowed by fear.

"We'll talk once we get outside. Let's get you signed out and I'm sure you'd agree… away from this place. We have some very important issues to discuss."

Zohra searched for a hidden message behind the woman's eyes, but failed to recognize anything of merit. She did catch one sign, as the woman whose name still remained a mystery stepped from behind the stroller to allow her to push it; the rightful owner of the children was now in charge. She followed her to the desk. The two signed the necessary papers and Zohra's property was returned, minus the wedding ring she'd given Sulaiman minutes before her arrest. After completing the business, Zohra trailed behind the stranger to a twin power turbo BMWi8. The moment her eyes sat on it, she knew she wanted one.

The twins were securely strapped in their car seats. Her instincts made her peer around before taking the passenger's side, yet for some reason she hadn't been in fear of her life or her babies' safety. From experience, she knew a professional had all the opportunities in the world to take them all out.

Zohra claimed her seat right before the turbo hummed, as the i8 was brought to life, and the vehicle pulled off without her knowing their destination. She was wise enough not to ask any questions, and knew it was a no-no to talk business in the car.

"Is this your car?" Zohra wanted to make small talk to keep her from going insane. The silence was killing her, and the need to be close to her babies was even greater. She hadn't even kissed them yet. There had been so many other distractions she'd forgotten to do so.

"This car belongs to a friend of your husband's friend," she answered, simply stated.

Zohra smiled. The female, whoever she was, had been well trained, but she knew behind that explosive sweetness was a mirage. She tried hard to avoid the awkwardness, but she desperately needed to gain some type of insight.

Sensing Zohra's patience slipping, she pulled out her cell phone, pushed a button then handed the device over.

After their salutations, the sound of Sulaiman's voice somewhat calmed her down. "Dee, I apologize for not being there, but as you know, it was urgent I fly to Rome. This matter has taken much longer than expected,"

Sulaiman said, then quickly corrected his folly, "I mean, *Zohra*. Jamal's dead."

"Jamal's dead?" She couldn't believe her ears. She knew how much her husband loved his brother, and the hell he'd gone through to secure his freedom.

He didn't want to repeat the words, so instead he simply replied, "I have to bring his body back home. If I leave him there, I'll have to bury my mother as well."

"What about the killer?"

Sulaiman tried to contain his emotions but found it very difficult to do so.

Zohra listened attentively. Her emotions were raw as well, especially after hearing her husband break down a couple of times.

Even he, had been clueless as to the circumstances surrounding the murder, but he did know who was responsible. He'd sworn a fury of vengeance that was unheard of to the human race, one so gruesome no man, woman or child would ever forget it.

Sulaiman had two friends he could call on. Jamal was helping out one of the friends who went by the name, Dice. It was Dice who caused an upheaval in Rome. The other was named Storm, and he was tracking down the killers who shot one of his best friends, leaving him dead. And if ever combined, God only knows the wrath these men would cause.

Tears stream down her soft, pale skin. It wasn't that of pleasant warmth she was feeling, but a scolding hot rage that ate at the core of her soul. She wished she were with him to console him and hold her husband in her loving arms. He needed to be held, but the reality of it all was that it would only be feasible once Jamal's killers were six-feet deep, rotting in concrete with soil tossed on top.

This led her to a decision which took no pondering or second-guessing. She didn't request, but instead demanded, the information to handle the problem so he could hurry home. He tried to put up an effective argument, being that she hadn't been 15 minutes from release, but sternly, she stuck to her guns. She added that time was of the essence, while simultaneously killing the tennis match debate, which in turn would give the female extra time to plot, plan and execute. This was an opportunity to kill two birds with one stone. She knew it sounded ridiculous coming from lips who only an hour ago praised the Lord, but her intentions were very clear……an assassination was about to take place in one of the worst of ways. *The dilemma she faced…..* She thought as her mind pondered on what lie ahead.

Zohra loathed unfinished tasks. The trials in her complicated life were already mounting, but she willed herself to remain focused. Crashing into an emotional ditch would prove fatal for all of them. As much as she wanted to be near her babies, she had to send them back to New York. There wasn't time for any distractions, and with them close by, that would definitely be the case. With that being noted, she asked the female to pull over to the nearest corner store, so she could put something in her growling stomach. She'd completely forgotten the fact that she'd skipped the breakfast meal.

Seeing a Mexican restaurant she'd heard of while in prison, Zohra quickly changed her mind. She pointed towards the sign and said, "There, that's the place I want to eat my first meal."

So much for cooking a meal, the female thought, as she smiled and replied, "Great choice."

Eying for anyone whose intention could be trailing them, she had been pretty sure they weren't followed. As she got out of the vehicle, she noticed the female had been conscious of the same thought. They managed to get the sleeping infants out of the car, and once the two smelled the aroma, they woke with their stomachs growling like their mother's.

The place was crowded, which was better to Zohra's liking. With luck, she found a table a family for six, a family had just left. She claimed it before the waitress even had a chance to clean it.

Once the table was cleaned a menu was provided. Shortly after, orders were taken and each woman took a child to feed. Zohra wanted to get to know the woman her husband so vehemently trusted with her children. She peered at her watch to remain conscious of the mark's flight hour. She knew the mark had fled from Rome and was flying into Oakland. Reminding herself of a few things on her agenda, she remembered to calculate the driving distance and add in transportation to the equation.

The waitress brought them fish tacos and the grubbing began. Zohra loved the West Coast dishes, hot and spicy just like her. While sitting enjoying the meal, along with the kids, she took the opportunity to get to know the female whom her children loved very much. She now understood Maria's concerns.

"It seems you know a lot about me and my family. And, its obvious Sulaiman trusts you. Please, tell me a little about yourself if you don't mind." She had previously noted the beautiful woman didn't have one of the boroughs accent, but clearly foreign.

"I don't mind at all." She smiled, and her pearly whites made Zohra remember her to-do list once home, a dentist trip among the top ten.

"My name is Ayesha BaQi."

"That's very beautiful."

"Thank you."

Zohra nodded. "Continue."

"I work for your husband as the nanny. I'm also their protector," she said with a confidence of one who was proud of both titles. She'd lived up to them well. "I was once homeless in Manshiyat Naser. I came to the States with a church group, even though I'm born muslima and white, here, I secured a permit to work. After six months, I returned back home."

It suddenly dawned on Zohra where she'd heard of the place from…..travelling aboard with her mother. "That's in Egypt, if I'm correct."

"Yes, that is correct. It's known as the 'Garbage City'."

"Is it true young children shift through trash to find scraps?"

"It is… I was one of those children." A moment of quietness came between the two.

"So, how did you meet Sulaiman?" she questioned as most curious or jealous women do.

"He saved my life, actually."

Zohra's eyebrows rose.

"He tends to do that a lot on a regular." She joked. Ayesha knew a lot about her, and she felt it only right that she know her personally as well, especially if she was going to remain a part of the family.

"As I've said, I had a work pass to be in the States, but I returned home because my adoptive parents were found dead. A home invasion is what investigators told me. Later, I found out my mother's lover had killed them in a jealous rage. Regardless of what happened, I was left homeless again."

"I'm sorry," Zohra mouthed sincerely.

Ayesha continued, "I managed to secure reentrance to the country, and with hard work, I became a legal citizen. The job I had was shut down for running an illegal enterprise, which sent me back to the streets within eight months of my stay. I was hungry, too ashamed to return to the church family for support. Anyway, I felt as if they were using me as a poster child to raise funds for their projects. I was passed around in a political orgy until I'd finally had enough. So, once again, I found myself on the rough and gritty streets of Charlotte, on the corners pestering people for handouts."

Zohra thought about one of her hadiths she memorized by the Prophet's household, *'Do know it that insistently begging questioning for the grant of need takes away the honor and causes incontinence, pain and suffering.'* Her mind snapped from the saying as her daughter Duaa's rattler soared across the table and into her brother's lap, who was being held by Ayesha. Ayesha handed the toy back to Zohra after wiping it clean with a wet-wipe and drying it with a napkin.

She went on to explain how the young dope boys constantly urged her to be their rider, promising riches and street clout, the fame of being a baller's main chick, titles she wouldn't see her body or soul for. Her pride wouldn't allow her to suck or fuck for a meal, so she went back to what she knew, eating out of the trash cans. The only difference in that was Americans were far more generous with their tossed out foods. Poverty and adversities she was all too familiar with. Countless times she'd tossed humiliation over her back.

One day, Sulaiman was exiting a store. He had just finished gassing up his vehicle and was on his way to handle some business in South Carolina, when she approached him for some change. Not pressed for time, he stared the beauty in the eyes. He held up a finger, then popped his trunk and dug in. He proceeded to pull out a small hand held vac. and handed it to her. The words he said were words she'd never forget. *"Don't ever ask a man for a hand-out. It's better to have the shame of work, than the disgrace of begging."* She said nothing. Instead, she took heed, as she began cleaning the seats and floor, contemplating on his words. Once she completed the small task, Sulaiman handed her a hundred dollar bill and told her to be careful in the streets. The memory had her touched.

"I stretched the money like a pair of jeans. I got me a hotel room, skipping the shelter I stayed in. For a change I was able to buy me something hot to eat from the kitchen, no disrespect to the soup kitchen, but I was just about burnt out on it. But, I'm grateful."

"That's understandable," Zohra acknowledged.

Ayesha paused a second before continuing. "As you know, a hundred dollars doesn't last very long. Sad and dejected, I found myself in my previous state yet again, thus making up my mind to comply to the drug dealers propositions and get paid." Zohra didn't judge her, but the change of expression let her know woman to woman, submitting disgrace was always a touchy subject for them. "I shoplifted something presentable to wear, and it was my first time stealing out of a department store. I despise a thief, but I understand situations can cloud ones better judgment. I took a sponge bath at a gas station restroom and didn't return to the shelter. My mission was to snag me a high class drug dealer, whatever that was. All I knew was that men loved my beauty, and I wasn't going to sell myself cheap. The highest bidder would purchase not just looks but my virginity." Now she realized that kind of thinking back then was insane.

"My God, you were a virgin!"

"I still am, thanks to your husband."

"That's a dark path. I've never had to travel before," Zohra replied sincerely. She shook her head knowing the grim outcome of such pitiful decisions millions of women make, almost daily in some form or another.

"I pray no one ever has too. Anyway, I hitch-hiked a ride back to the block, determined to change my life. I felt I deserved a life of luxury, just as the next female. I saw women all around me who were driving in style, wearing expensive clothing, purchasing someone else's Brazilian hair for $1500 on up, while I had good hair texture and length naturally; dark, thick and oily like men love it. My nails weren't done, but they were long, neat, clean and natural. These women…not being racist, but I saw they felt unhappy being themselves, not proud of their own beautiful black skin, they felt the need to imitate other races to make themselves feel and look beautiful. In the early 2000's there were just as many black blondes as there were whites."

Zohra couldn't contain her laughter. "I could never understand that myself. And as you said, *not being racist*, but I could never see myself wearing an Afro wig to make me look like a beautiful black woman."

Ayesha agreed and returned back to the original subject. She went on to tell about how she was a young and naïve virgin, fearful of what her world had come to. At least in her country she had family. Here, she had nothing, and the little she had was sent back to help her brother and sister, whom she so desperately wanted to get over here to the States. She wanted desperately to change their condition from that of orphans to one of an American dream and opportunity.

She targeted a young hustler, who, around the way was labeled a pretty boy. She didn't care about him being black. Hell, her rich olive tone was several shades darker than his light-skinned complexion, which in and of itself, was a shade above a sun-tanned Caucasian. The handsome, smooth, baby-fine D-boy, who was *getting paper* as they called it, wasn't seen as most guys. You'd never see him with a car load of females. Occasionally, she'd notice one or two teenagers flirting with him then they'd vanish inside his apartment for 15 to 30 minutes or so, but that was about it. She observed the cycle for three weeks until she caved in.

One day he invited her to come in out of the cold. They had been talking and like any eager teen, she fell for it and followed him like a true dummy.

He did some sort of secret knock and someone on the other side of the door unbolted it, and an equally handsome tall guy with dreadlocks to his ass, stood with a 9 mm in hand, eyeing both sharply, before relaxing and stepping to the side. Two other unknown men glanced up at them from behind a table then went straight back to bagging up the drugs on the table for distribution. They were shirtless and she prayed they had something on below, shit seemed gay to her….just saying.

D-Red led her to a back room. Without any words or delays, he started fumbling with the buttons on her blouse. Things were going too fast, but due to her lack of experience, she didn't know if this was right or wrong. Since he'd stripped of his clothing and was now tearing into hers, all she knew was it was about to happen.

"He didn't waste any time, did he?" Zohra stated, and kissed Duaa's fat cheek.

"You can say that again." She laughed. "I remember his penis was long, thick, and dripping clear liquid." She laughed again. "His eyes, which were a greenish color, turned the hue of embarrassment. Luckily, we were interrupted by a commotion which followed by an uneasy silence. David tried to reach for his gun, but was stopped short by a roundhouse boot to the chin, which landed him in a heap across the room. Right then and there, I knew I had to learn to defend myself."

That could only be one person, Zohra thought, as she smiled and replied, "I know who that was."

"Sulaiman stood there staring me directly in my eyes. Here I was, in all my glory as naked as the day I entered the world, and it was as if he didn't even notice me. I felt so ashamed, and then I grew angry."

"He didn't notice you; considering your dilemma. He's not driven by the flesh, although he is a man with needs."

"I understand that now since I know him, but to a female naked….," she paused, "to think he didn't take a notice of me crashed my, already fragile, self-esteem. He told me to put on my clothes and go get in the car, like he was my big brother or daddy. I definitely protested. I crossed my arms and pouted my lips child-like. David stirred and again tried to reach for his gun. Without so much as taking his eyes off of me, David's stupidity got him one in the forehead. It was at that point, I fainted."

Zohra didn't mean to laugh, but she visualized the entire scene. *That was my Sulaiman all right, coming to the rescue!* She thought as she smiled in admiration. She had never witnessed this Sulaiman, but saw it in his lovely, yet deadly, brown eyes.

Ayesha proceeded in telling her that when she woke up, she was lying on Sulaiman's couch at his condo. She remembered thinking it all had been a terrible dream. The condo was immaculate and spotless, unlike the squalid homes and shacks she'd requested. Ayesha inhaled the fragrance of potpourri and myrrh; she didn't want to stop inhaling. Sulaiman sat on a nearby sofa, talking on the phone, as if nothing had ever happened. He watched her go from a groggy, confused state, to one of shock, wondering if the place she was in belonged to him.

"You can thank me later. But right now, you need to get something in your stomach. It growled loud enough to scare my dogs," he'd said, and then pointed at two Doberman pinchers posted by the front door.

"I couldn't believe he said I could thank him later. He had just lemon juiced a man and I was supposed to thank him? I was about to call the cops." She laughed, as she recalled the thought. "Then he hit me with those four letter words no human being wants to ever hear. *Your friend had A.I.D.S. and he didn't mind generously dishing it out to young, attractive and ignorant ladies. He's been passing it around like government assistance,*" she said, trying to sound like Suliaman. Her imitation caused Deen to look up at her. "Still to this day, he hasn't mentioned repayment, or my body. The only thing he's required of me is my loyalty, and *that* he'll forever have."

"That's good, because loyalty to him is loyalty to me. I hope you agree?"

"Totally," she replied sincerely.

"One last thing, Ayesha….."

"Speak."

"Have you ever wanted to sleep with my husband?" Zohra questioned with a serious expression masking her face.

Without stutter or hesitation she replied, "What woman in their right mind wouldn't? But the loyalty I've just spoken about comes by not ruining a bond that's unbreakable, because of flesh. So, I stay in my lane and that's well enough for me. And, I'm proud to say, I'm still a virgin thanks to Sulaiman."

Zohra nodded. She approved of the honesty, which was truly needed, especially living in her house.

Chapter Three

The more the women conversed, the more Zohra realized Sulaiman had indeed mentioned her. Upon completing their meals, Zohra made Ayesha promise that if anything should ever happen to her, she'd continue to take care of her family. She needed Ayesha to distinctively understand what it was she was requesting. Should she die, she needed to know that Ayesha would marry her husband and hold the family down.

Knowing it was a vow she intended to uphold, Ayesha promised. She also assured Zohra that whatever it was she planned to do, she was more than confident, Zohra could pull it off. After all, she was the alleged daughter of the Bronx's drug cartel leader, more than capable of handling herself.

Zohra knew Sulaiman wouldn't have just trusted anyone unless he explicitly had faith in their abilities. There were a list of people he could have sent to pick her up, mainly Kendrick or one of his people, and left the kids home until she arrived, this let her know, Ayesha was special. She was glad to have Ayesha as a part of the family, which made her decide to surround herself with new trustworthy people which were rare these days. Zohra prayed Ayesha's attributes would prevail, time would only tell.

Zohra wrapped things up because every second counted and she wasn't about to let Suliaman down. She needed recovery time for unplanned errors, purchasing or securing the necessary equipment, transportation, and stakeout time. She despised going into situations blindly. The female had to know someone was coming for her. And going into unfamiliar territory, was as dangerous as chewing on broken glass.

It was time to make her move. Although she hated to go, she made sure Ayesha was on the same page as she was. She made Ayesha repeat everything word-for-word without so much as a glance at the napkin she had written the note on. Satisfied, she kissed her twins. Ayesha gave her the address and phone number to the location she'd be staying until they headed back to New York. She then slid her several credit cards, a wad of cash and a single trip first class airplane ticket to the Big Apple, before leaving.

Zohra stayed behind and peered out of the restaurant's window. After watching Ayesha secure the kids inside the car, she sipped on hot, dark, sugarless coffee, and went over different scenarios, taking into consideration the unexpected. She couldn't afford to be implicated in any atrocities. Kidnapping, breaking and entering, a possible 187 or perhaps even 2, depending on how things turned out; with a list of charges like that, it would most definitely be lights out for life. She downed the last of her coffee before vanishing from the restaurant, leaving behind a tip and the pink hijab.

She walked three blocks before spotting a white, '64 Chevy Impala low-rider, trimmed in black waiting at the intersection for the light to change. The driver kept his alert eyes on his surroundings in case someone had intentions of a jack-move. Shyly, she bent over giving him a glimpse of a perfect gap shot. She knew with a hot ass like hers, any man would find it hard to resist looking at the curvaceous figure. Just as she thought, the driver ogled at the upside down, heart shaped rump, as she stripped off her sneakers to massage her foot as if it were sore, *acting at its finest.*

She slid the New Balance back on smoothly. Several guys peered out of a barber shop window, wondering who would let such a lovely woman foot it, nevertheless, all by her lonesome. Zohra peered around as if she was lost and proceeded to walk on. She was hoping he'd think with the wrong head, as men usually tend to do, and snatch the bait.

He grabbed the hook with teeth of lust, and held on for dear life, "Excuse me!" the Hispanic American called from behind the wheel. Zohra continued on, as if no one had said a word. "Come on, don't be like that."

She spun to face the cute, but slightly, obese male.

"I don't want to come off as a stalker or anything, but I noticed you rubbing your feet. Do you wanna ride somewhere? It doesn't look like you're gonna make it in those shoes."

There wasn't anything wrong with her foot wear; in fact, they were as comfortable as ever. It was all a part of the lure to get inside of his car and take it by force, along with any other possessions of value which could be used to her advantage later on down the line.

Zohra sneered evil-eyed, then said, "How do I know you're not some creepy perv or stalker?"

Right away, he noticed the east coast accent. He knew it well, and his mother had been raised in Spanish Harlem.

"Are you serious? Do I look like I gotta take pussy from a bitch?" He vulgarly retorted, offended.

His attitude didn't faze her in the least bit, and she replied, "Most rapists appear to be the innocent looking types." She laughed. "But, you do appear to be more hustler than rapist."

"You damn skippy, I grind hard in these here streets of L.A."

With that final comment, she made her way over to the vehicle. Once inside, she noticed a burner halfway concealed for easy access of reach. "Let's go. I need to get away. My car broke down. I drove over 3,000 miles to see my cheating ass boyfriend and caught him with a man."

"What! He's gay?"

"Duh, unless they have a new name for it when a man has a dick up another man's shitter, I would guess it's still called that."

"Damn, girl. So, you're saying the two of you had a long distance relationsh....?" Before he could get the words out, she'd cut him off mid-sentence.

"Are you going to crank this ride up, or stay parked on the curb and ask 20 questions like my homeboy 50?"

Realizing she was right, he started the car.

"Just drive, I don't care where we go. You smoke Cali bud?"

"You the police?"

"If I was, you wouldn't be riding dirty with a loaded gun," she responded sharply. This time she acted as though she was offended. "I hate cops with a passion. But if you need further convincing, find us a place somewhere behind one of these stores and I'll prove it."

Not fully comprehending what she was hinting at, she made it easier for him to understand by unzipping his fly and extracting his average sized cock from his boxers. She began stroking it to life, as she calculated his length to be at least six inches shorter than her husband's rod. However, it was thicker in width, fat and uncircumcised, which really didn't matter to her one bit. She'd never find out what he could do with it, nor would he ever experience the bliss of being in her tight, juicy cunt which had been on ice for far too long. As she bent to give him head, he whipped the low rider behind a ruined department store that had gotten destroyed in the king's riots.

As the Chevy parked, she spat the razor from her mouth and did a *Bobbitt* on his manhood. Chunking the dismembered flesh to the concrete, something told her to keep the razor. She'd kept it on her for protection while incarcerated. It was an old trick from her youthful days while growing up in New York in the buck-fifty era.

When she reached for his 9 mm. and let off a single round to his upper thigh, a scream more feminine than male was released from his lungs. "If you don't comply with my demands, the next one will be in your temple. So, shut the fuck up and listen!" She threatened in a raised tone.

To no avail, he squeezed what was left of his member, trying to stop the bleeding. The gangsta in him disappeared, as he begged not to be killed. Foolishly, he tried to wrestle the weapon from her while threatening to kill her once he got his hands on her. The risk proved he wasn't the sharpest saw in the barn. Zohra told him to take a number. His last words had been quoted to her multiple times, and so were the words she'd said. Luckily, no one had kept their word, as of yet.

She didn't want to kill him. All he had to do was follow her instructions, but his hard head made a soft skull, as another bullet entered him, this time to his chest.

Tears wailed in his uncertain eyes, unassured of his current fate. He pleaded, and things were serious. "Please, don't leave me like this!" He motioned to the area of his body which bled the most.

Zohra peered down to her damaged work, "I don't plan to," she said, as she raised the weapon, now eye level.

"Oh, God," he shouted, as he cried out the sinner's plea. The deafening gun blast shortened any other words he may have had, and his lifeless corpse slumped over to the driver's door.

Working on instincts, not emotions, the killer in Zohra had come back as if it had never left, a pesky shadow lost in the sunlight. Quickly, she looted his pockets and snatched his billfold from his back pocket. In haste, she jammed it in her own pocket without surveying its contents. She did a swift sweep of the vehicle and found a sawed off shotgun under the driver's seat.

"That's LA for you," she murmured, "no other streets like it in the world."

Blood was at a minimum, which was good considering the multiple gunshot wounds inflicted. Zohra took off her top layer shirt, and after pushing him out onto the concrete, did a quick wipe-down of the vehicle. She eased off as if nothing had ever happened.

My first day out and a kill under my belt already, so much for being scared straight, this is turning out to be one hell of a day, she thought to herself. She drove about six miles away from the crime scene and stopped at a convenience store to purchase a map.

Block huggers posted in front of the store, each one stared at her oddly as she exited the vehicle. She made sure her tool was visible in case someone felt lucky or stupid. By the looks, the guys were well aware of the owner, and with that in mind, she planned to get in and out as fast as possible. *Some inquiring mind may decide to snoop, and it seems that dudes are worse than females these days when it comes to nosiness,* she thought to herself as she glanced around. An open challenge was given to those who stared, daring one to test her, but no one accepted it. They all took notice of the stern look on her face, as she pushed the glass door open and made her way to the counter.

"I need a map of California," she said nonchalantly to the Korean store clerk, "or, Oakland."

"One or two?" he asked.

"Now, why would I need two of the same map?" She mumbled, "One, please," she replied paying for a cold Pepsi and a bag of plain chips to go with it. *Maybe he thought one each?* She pondered on his question and decided to cut him some slack.

"$10.95"

She shook her head, peeled off a $20 dollar bill and left him with the change. Apparently he needed it more than her charging those outrageous prices.

Zohra sat in the vehicle with the 9mm resting comfortably on her lap. She studied the map studiously, allowing her eyes to scan the contents for the quickest route to Oakland. She dived into the Pepsi and chips, devouring both as if she hadn't eaten in days; somehow, killing always made her hungry. She had penciled in the better route mentally. Tossing the trash aside, she hit the highway fiercely, driving non-stop. She was careful so as not to break any traffic laws that could cause her to get pulled over. The drive was as murderous as she'd been.

The kill weighed heavily on her heart. She wanted to tie him up and leave him but he charged at her and that had sent her into attack mode. Now the Qu'ranic verses were repeatedly admonishing her. *"Whosoever kills someone is as though he has killed all of humanity… and whosoever saves a life is as though he has saved all of humanity…"* The powerful words resounded throughout her mind, for she knew it was only right to listen and heed the words of her Lord, but her sincerity and dedication to her husband clouded her better judgement. What was she to do?

Chapter Four

Zohra didn't want this life anymore, for herself or for Sulaiman, who was in Rome helping his best friend take on the mafia. He too struggled with his faith versus the loyalty to family and friends, and those in need hindered him from being loyal to his Creator.

Zohra began to recite the 99 attributes of God. She had to keep herself grounded and maintain everything she fought for, along with her dedication to her Lord. She realized that she had found herself engulfed in the flames of sins already, and more was sure to follow.

The drive to Oakland was a success, besides a few minor traffic incidences which slowed her progress, but nevertheless, she arrived in ample time. Zohra was mentally drained beyond words, but she had a mission to conduct and wasn't about to let her husband down.

The female target was responsible for Jamal's death and she had to pay; there were no questions about that, a life for a life, no blood money. She used the cellphone looted from the dead man's pocket to call the number given to her by Ayesha to reach Sulaiman. She needed to ensure the location and address.

He picked up on the second ring.

"I'm here. I need the address," she spoke, a little over a whisper in a shaky voice.

Sulaiman gave his wife the necessary information. The sound of his voice made her want to board the next flight to Rome. She abruptly ended the call, knowing not to stay on the line too long. She broke the phone up, and scattered its pieces in a dumpster at a Jack in a Box. With extreme caution, she went straight to work, logging down the necessary info for the job.

Thirty-minutes later she was parked a few yards away from the condo, taking notes on who came in and out, the traffic of the surrounding apartments, the different escape routes, and collecting Intel on the alleged female whom no one seemed to know. The victim's death would be swift and speedy then she'd return home to her twins. *Twins*....she loved the sound of it, especially since she shared them with Sulaiman.

Zohra was tired mentally, which to her was worse than being tired physically. Had time permitted, she would have checked into a nearby hotel, but there wasn't time to rest. She didn't want to be seen on a hotel security camera and definitely wasn't about to go to the hood and slum it out in an infested roach motel. She had to be careful, for the streets didn't love anybody, so it was best to lay low and stay out of sight, because although her beauty had been a blessing, true indeed, it had also been a curse at times. Guys were always eyeing her; they stopped her with ridiculous pick-up lines and absurd promises of giving her the world.

Zohra was glad she'd left her hijab back in L.A. There was no way she could kill with it on. No, *it* wasn't to be worshipped; only God, but her conscious wouldn't allow her to wear it. A mere cloth one would say, yet, the fact remained, it represented her faith, a faith founded upon peace, not terrorism or violence, in which she was about to display. *Hypocrite,* she thought, a shame to the religion she felt.

❦

Zohra drove to an abandoned house a few blocks away, mindful of the time her husband had informed her of the soon-to-be victim's arrival. She decided to dress the part, and since this was an assassination, it was only fitting all black attire should be worn, so she made her way to nearest surplus store. After gathering the necessary gear, she made the purchase, kept quiet the entire time, handed the cashier the money he requested, and again, she left the change.

Night fall descended almost thief-like. Usually with something of this nature, night would have taken forever to come, but the hour had arrived.

After ravishing down a meal at McDonalds, she made her way back, but not before driving across the street to a closed mall to inspect the trunk of the vehicle. *How stupid of me,* she thought, *not to have searched it sooner.* She popped the trunk and proceeded to move a few things around. *Bam!* Right in front of her eyes sat two kilos, wrapped tightly, ready for distribution, along with several guns in a gym bag. *Boy, was I slipping,* she thought again, glad she'd taken the time to search.

Zohra rode around in a jacked car with more dope than the law allowed and enough guns to wage a small arms war, not that many actually, but you get the picture, she was loaded. She grabbed the bag, glad she worked out because the weight taxed her tone biceps and her to-die for back arms. The bag was placed in the front passenger's seat as she continued thinking to herself. *The first dealer I see, I'm putting him on.*

Just as she hopped in, an SUV pulled up, bumping music loud enough to shake the carwash foundation. Zohra got back out of the Chevy and walked over to the black SUV, and the window on the driver's side slid down like thongs at a strip club, so did the music.

"What it do, Sexy?" His Texas drawl was thick and lovely like those Austin beauties.

"I'm good," Zohra replied then got straight to the point. "You see that 64 over there?"

The driver nodded. "Nice."

"It is, but it's not mine. It's a dead man's car." She pulled her shirt to reveal the 9mm.

"Damn, baby girl, beautiful and deadly," he said, eyeing the heat as she concealed it.

"A hell of a combination, but why are you telling us all this? I ain't try'na be no co-defendant. Feel me?"

Zohra gave his words no merits. "I'm trying to get rid of it, and I got a deal on two bricks of raw uncut coke. I'll let them both fly for 50."

Both men stared at one another then back to her, as if this were some sort of "Punk'd" T.V. episode. Her stern facial expression showed it wasn't a game nor was it a show, but what it was, was the makings of a legit business deal.

The driver shifted in his seat nervously, recalling that just minutes prior she'd flashed a weapon, even though the two were packing themselves. In killer Cali, no one was to be underestimated, so it quashed any insane ideas they may have had in their pea brains. The driver was certain about *that* life, and this would be a guaranteed put on.

"Prove you not a pig," he said, face etched in stone.

"Tell him, to get out of the vehicle."

"What, hell no!" the light-skinned passenger barked, in a shocked tone.

"You said you wanted proof, so hop your ass out dude," she demanded, attempting to sound as street-like as the two of them appeared to be.

"Man, raise yo' ass up fool. Let's see what she has to offer."

Not knowing what was in store for him, the passenger, hesitantly, exited the vehicle, shaking his head as he mumbled, "It better not be no bullshit."

"Come here. I'm not going to waste any more of my time," she said, adding what she thought to be a hint of intimidation in her voice.

"I don't know who the fuck you think you….." he started to say but was instantly taken aback by Zohra's next movement.

Zohra pulled him roughly towards her and pushed the 9mm. into his gut; a pop sounded, followed by a bitch-cry, a guaranteed shit-bag indeed.

The guy staggered forward as his Oakland A's fitted fell to the ground, almost simultaneously followed by his body, but Zohra quickly caught him. She helped him to the Impala, entertaining a slew of cuss words in her ear.

By now, the driver of the SUV was so stunned at the thugged-out red head, his eyes bugged out of his head. Her actions caused him to react and snatch his .38 special, just in case. He helped her put his partner inside the Impala on the passenger's side, and placed his hat back on his head, snuggly.

"Bruh, don't let her get away with this shit! Don't… listen to her," he coughed out, knowing greed had been the cause of many ties being severed.

The .38 was placed to his chest and a small hole was made by the single squeeze of a trigger. Smoke escaped the dime-sized hole in the blue flannel shirt, adding to the other hole made in the soft twilled fabric. He tucked the rod back inside his waist band and asked, "Now, where were we?"

"Two bricks, trade vehicles and let's not forget the cash."

"Deal," he replied as he stuck out his hand, "I'm Kris."

"Who cares?"

He smiled.

The deal went through smoothly, and Zohra waited patiently while Kris, *if* that was truly his name, called his girl to bring the cash. She told him if anything looked funny, she'd kill him with the quickness; somehow, he believed every word.

A Carolina blue, F-150 Raptor pulled up with a white female who slide out of the driver's seat carrying a tote bag. She was white and her long, beautiful, brown hair blew with the light breeze, leaving a lingering fragrance that smelled like a once-squeezed perfume bottle of your favorite scent. The momentarily shock at the sight of the lovely red head took her by surprise, but this was California, nothing was supposed to shock you. There was no exchanging of pleasantries, strictly business.

    Minutes later, Zohra watched the couple pull off in the Raptor and she hopped inside the SUV, its engine running, and left the car wash. She drove off cautiously, with her fingers on the trigger. She needed to be sure her mind wasn't playing tricks on her. Although she'd left behind the '64, she still felt as if she were being shadowed.

Chapter Five

Zohra parked the SUV a few yards down from the condo. Still feeling as if she'd been followed, she made a few circles around the block until she had been sure no one had trailed the SUV. She entered and the building was relatively clear. She walked up to the elevator, calm like a spring day. Several suspecting eyes stared at her lethal dress wear and fitted ball cap pulled tightly over her forehead. Once the elevator doors slid open, for some strange reason her heart rate spiked, and this had never happened to her before.

She would never admit it, but she got a personal thrill from jobs such as this, she held no remorse for the one responsible for the murderer who killed her brother-in-law.

The ride was smooth, and as the box crept to its destination, so did her heart. The elevator rested on the respective floor and peeled open slowly. She took in a deep breath, then exhaled and stepped into the hallway with her black gloved hand on her weapon of choice, the .380 from the duffle bag she'd just slid out of her wristband. Quickly, Zohra concealed the piece.

A hot, black hunk walked in her direction and stopped directly in front of her, "Zohra?"

Her eyes stretched in shock, she was beyond words. "Who are you?" She put her hand close to the burner.

Acutely aware if what her intentions and capabilities were, he responded quickly, taking over the situation by grabbing her by the arm and leading her back inside the elevator. She stood frozen in her tracks.

"I'm Storm. Your husband sent me." The two watched the velvet doors close. "The job has been taken care of. You can return to New York."

Zohra breathed out slowly. Thank God she didn't have to shed blood again. A burden lifted as they rode the rest of the way in silence. *Return to New York?* That was music to her ears.

Finally, she had the pleasure of meeting the man her husband had frequently talked about as a brother, more than a friend. What puzzled her was Storm's personal presence, there had to be a reason behind it.

The doors open and they were now back on the main floor, where two extremely beautiful women unknown to her, walked up to them and asked her to follow them. When she spun around to thank Storm, he had disappeared, almost as if into thin air. His next mission was to gather the building's security tapes from upstairs. An autopsy report would show evidence of blunt force trauma as the room blazed, a death ruled from smoke inhalation.

Still, no words were spoken as the three women made their way through the lobby and outside. They sat in a black A8, purring like a regal panther in front of the building. Behind its wheel sat a white sexy female who could have easily walked a runaway.

Zohra accepted a bag from her, which had been filled with clothing from JNY.com. She sat up front amazed the correct size had been given by the hottie with the bold graphic eyes. She hadn't turned her head from the road as passers watched Zohra strip off her clothes and replace them with a red Jill Stuart skirt, matching colored blouse and a pair of Stuart Weitzman boots, which she slid on. Zohra loved the footwear.

The SUV had been removed from its parked spot. She noticed and wondered if Storm had anything to do with it. Further into the heart of downtown, the driver made a stop at a red light, and as an old woman pushed a shopping cart across the street, the woman with the junk filled cart was called to the driver's side. Zohra handed her the assassin gear and a hundred dollar bill. The toothless smile showed her appreciation as the black luxury ride sped on off without its occupants ever looking back.

Shortly thereafter, Zohra was driven to the airport, a flight scheduled to the place she called home. Anxious to get back to the home she'd built from the ground up, to her children and await the arrival of her husband. God's will she prayed, hoping he'd make it back to her and the children safely, from the Eternal City. The women saw Zohra off and returned back to Storm who had urgent business in Las Vegas.

The last time Zohra had been on a plane, it had been far from a bitter sweet experience. The feds swarmed her, whisking her off to an awaiting helicopter, heavily guarded, to an unknown location where she was aggressively interrogated to no end. Knowing her legal rights, she opt the right to remain silent, requesting to use the phone so she could call legal representation. Her private on-call attorney had been in Oklahoma attending a game, and within minutes after the urgent call, he was on the first plane out to Los Angeles to see his client.

Zohra, while sitting comfortably in her first class window seat, couldn't help but think of the staggeringly beautiful Storm, not in a sexual way, although she couldn't control her wondering mind; the black ghost was very organized and professional. The handsomely dark-skinned man with strong cheeks and chin stood tall and confidentially made goosebumps scatter all over her body by his mere presence. Indeed, her heart belonged to Sulaiman, but she hadn't met a man of Storm's nature throughout her travels, nor anyone who'd come remotely close.

The cast of lovely, well-trained, all female clique were discipline and deadly. She could see her as a part of his flock, submissive in all ways. This made her think about her own cartel which was in need of cleansing. The undisciplined personnel was a headache in and of itself, not to mention the weak snitches who she had to constantly whack off because of their broken loyalties. The mounting burdens buckled her shoulders, often-times leaving her wondering how she put up with it all, but the lifestyle of mayhem had at one time come with ease, as if tying her shoes, or yet, even simpler, breathing. Not today, snitching came easy; as soon as the cops stuffed them inside a cruiser, the lips would run a marathon.

She vowed to give up the life, but found it very difficult, far more difficult than mere words on her tongue and heart. Everyone who got involved with the lifestyle knew exiting came with a heavy price, one many couldn't afford to pay, and many who already thought she didn't belong in the current position would definitely test her gangsta, and they'd find out the task wouldn't be so easy. A horrible death they'd meet, one with a .45 slug to the forehead.

Sometime during the flight, Zohra drifted off, finally dreaming about her African lover who was halfway across the world gunning it out in the streets, the madness… *When will it ever stop*? She pondered. She even thought about the vehicle the women got rid of. Storm's women were top notch professional to say the least.

The plane landed and that all too familiar nervousness which had accompanied her as of late, returned with a vengeance. Lately, it had become a bosom buddy, far from the cool, calm and collective image she portrayed amongst her peers. Her faith also kept her aware of the actions. The knowledge of atoning and punishment for the evilness done by her didn't help matters one bit, which weighed heavily on her psyche.

The sight of the New York skyline, its tall and glorious buildings came into view. The iron-eagle soared over clouds, descending slowly with its practice poise until its landing gear touched the concrete runway. *New York City….*

Zohra peered around the numerous hues of faces, all sizes, shapes, and colors, the 'Melting Pot'. She was more than happy to be home, but don't get it wrong, she loved the beautiful weather of sunny California, its magnificent palm trees, breathtaking oceans and its unmatchable Hollywood, but to Zohra, there wasn't a place on earth like her New York, New York.

Flabbergasted, her hands flew to her wide-open mouth. It was great that she didn't have any luggage, for it would have been scattered all over the area.

Sulaiman stood a short distance away with his hands jammed in his pockets with an uncharacteristic smile on his lovely, African face. He was flanked by Ayesha who held Duaa, and her housekeeper turned best friend with her son. Tears wailed up in her eyes upon recognition, and she tried everything humanly possible to keep from dashing but it was impossible to control the impulse. She sprinted like an Olympic medalist to her family and found herself embraced in a tight group hug. Tears of happiness streamed down her soft pale skin. *Oh, what a day….*

Zohra squeezed her husband not wanting to let go of him. He looked immaculate in his three-piece suit and imported dress shoes. Storm had rubbed off on him. She loved a man in a suit. He smelled so good, she buried her nose in his warm flesh and felt the effects of her closeness, as his erection showed he was equally glad to have her back with them. Her nude lips on his, and the sight by those who passed by made their hearts soften. Everyone wanted that special someone to love.

Zohra kissed her children, then her African husband, damn the rules about privacy and public affection. She had missed the hell out of him, and every single day, she found herself miserable without him by her side. Those familiar stares came, this time she welcomed them, she wanted, *no needed,* the world to know the love she had for this man. Had she not believed in God's oneness, she'd find herself at his black feet worshipping him daily. Reluctantly, she let loose of the embrace and couldn't wait to get home, strip, soak and make love, yes, in that order.

The stretch Mercedes Benz limo awaited her presence, as the driver held the door open for them all to file inside. Yet, another surprise awaited her, her best male friend, Kendrick, and his soon to be wife, sat inside with big joyous smiles across their faces.

"Welcome home, Snowflakes," Kendrick said, and then gave her a hug.

Over his shoulder she peered at her husband for approval. In her faith, besides males in her family, she wasn't to show affection with another man, only her husband. At first, she struggled with it, that is, until Sulaiman broke it down and it made perfect sense and logic. Most male friends end up making some type of move on the female behind her lover's back when they catch the female in a vulnerable state, and some even get so close, they listen to the friend's advice more than their lovers. At one point in her life, the latter proved to be true.

Zohra clung to her lover as they played with the twins. *Can one ever be so happy? Why do moments like these have to end?* This was her paradise on earth.

Her heart skipped beats when the electric gates with S&X on them slid open, as the security guard waved them on through. She hadn't seen old man Malcolm in over a year. She could tell he'd known she was inside, and by the smile on his face, glad to have her home. She made a mental note to have a private party thrown just for the workers who patiently stood by and remained loyal.

Zohra couldn't get out of the vehicle fast enough, a hot shower beckoned her and she wasn't about to dare deny it.

All staff on deck waited out front to greet the lady of the house, some faces were new, additions made by Sulaiman, and old ones who she considered dedicated and faithful.

After the hugs, kisses and handshakes, she entered the mansion only to be caught off guard.

"Surprise!!" a rowdy bunch of family and friends cheered.

Overwhelmed by the abundance of love, she turned toward her husband, whom she walked over to and hugged. More tears as the gathering clapped, glad she was released from her incarcerated state. With a warm kiss to the face, Sulaiman disappeared upstairs to leave her alone with the company that missed her so dearly, plus, he wasn't one for large crowds.

"Oh my gosh, Temptation! Where've you been?" she asked her friend. Her tone resonated surprise, according to word on the streets she was said to be dead.

As always, Temptation had made a grand entrance and everyone's head turned at the sight of the fabulous diva.

"Rehab, darling, do I look glamourous?" She spun around. "Not bad for someone who got shot and had an overdose on heroin, huh."

"Yes, as always," Zohra said then kissed both cheeks thinking, *overdose?*

"I'll talk to you later. There are some fine men in here and I need to do some scouting."

"I guess some things never change." Zohra giggled.

"Of course not, especially when it comes to men and money. Who doesn't like M&M's?" With that, Temptation sauntered off to a group of major figures.

Zohra thought about the Qau'ranic words. *And He it is who hath made you (His) vicegerent in the earth and raised some of you above others in grades that He may try you in what He gave you; verily thy Lord is quick in the requital (of evil) and (you) verily He is the Oft-Forgiving, the Merciful.*

Family or not, those guys were dangerous, and Temptation, even more so.

"Darling, I really need to speak with you privately, this new you, I don't understand." The voice of her Aunt punched her in the ears.

Zohra witnessed the concern from the worried posture. "My sister must be turning in her grave," she spat, referring to the interracial marriage.

Zohra held her peace. "We'll talk." She replied softly, "Right now, isn't a great time."

"I see he already has you turning against the family," she huffed, even though she knew her niece to be right; it wasn't a great time. "As soon as this circus is over," She waved her hand to express the individuals inside the mansion. "Get in touch with me. Better yet I'll be back tomorrow at 9:00 a.m. sharp." Her husband, quiet

William of 40 years, helped her into a fur coat then departed.

Zohra knew her Aunt didn't want to put her lips on her due to Sulaiman, which was fine with her. She also knew her Aunt would come full blast, and she was 100% ready to combat all the negativity tossed at her. But somehow, that brief conversation had drained her, but she refused to let it dampen her spirits. *The party must go on.* She thought and sighed to herself; she somehow managed to re-energize as she tended to her company. It was a little after four in the morning and the gathering was still very much alive.

Antonio War, Zohra's cousin, who against her words, continued the family business of pushing Mexican black tar heroin throughout the city, had multiplied the number of workers, boasting well over 125 drivers assigned to various locations, making it simple to purchase. With just a phone call a driver would be at your door within minutes of the call like a dedicated pizza delivery guy.

"Antonio, I gave explicit instructions to stop sells and delivery of all drugs, and gave six months grace period to clean up all business transactions, now I return to find out you're the leader of the cartel?"

"Everyone says you're soft, that when you married the black guy, he poisoned you into neglecting your true calling. There's even talk about harm coming to him."

"You barely know anything about the business," she said, not missing his words.

"Dee, I'm not some track-mark junkie from the back alley, nor some block-hugger pushing twenties from a chopstick tube. While they had you rotting in a cell, I made this business nourish into a powerful organization that's untouchable. Not only do we deal heroin and coke, I've got connections with OxyContin and Vicodin, with sells grossing more than the heroin and cocaine combined. A dollar each milligram," he explained. "That's $160 bucks for two 80mg pills. No shorts. I'm raking it in." He boasted.

Had Zohra not let things go, she would have been proud of him, but he went against her orders, so did the rest. Who cares if people think she's soft, but the threats against Sulaiman, she wasn't about to take lightly.

"Who's talking about my husband?"

"Just word on the streets, I doubt it's anything serious. Most just upset you've married a Black man, who I might add… happens to be cool," he said with sincerity.

Zohra noted the sincerity in his words. "Look, I'm not giving you my blessing, but I will say this, if you ever need advice or help, as family… I'm here for you. My faith has been the one and only constant in my life and has brought me from this devastating and traumatic lifestyle I've lived."

"But Dee, you're a War. It's all we do, but I respect the change, now mom, that's an entire different subject."

"Tell me about it. She wants to meet with me later on. I'm glad I got some sleep on the plane. She will be here bright and early."

Temptation interrupted their talk. "Excuse me handsome, but may I borrow my best friend?" Temptation knew Antonio well; the two fooled-around a few times when she had fall-outs with Zohra's brother. Sadly, she had a few immediate families left, even a couple in attendance she chatted with.

Antonio gave both women a hug, and then found his way to a group of women who were single and searching.

Temptation's words went through one ear and out the other. Zohra's mind was totally on Antonio. It was true about the drug business. She had read it for herself, more middle-class buyers than junkies in crack houses. But, little did he know, the DEA Agents kept watch on him for weeks and soon an arrest would be imminent.

"Dee, did you hear anything I said?"

"Oh, sorry, my mind was on Antonio. I fear for him."

"Girl, he'll be alright. He's been around enough dealers to know how to move in a closet filled with vipers," she encouraged.

"Do you have a place to accommodate your needs for the time you're here?"

"Glad you asked. I was just about to let you know I was leaving to get a hotel. I'll see you la…"

"You're staying here with me."

"But…"

"No but's. I won't take no for an answer."

From out of nowhere Sulaiman stepped in and hugged both women. "Please, be our guest. I have tickets for us to attend the All Star games at the Madison Square Garden tomorrow."

Temptation had prayed for this moment, she really did want to stay, especially in Sulaiman's company. She knew he was a major figure, and just to be in his midst of A-list ballers, nothing but good could come of it, plus, the weather had the airlines with a slew of cancellations and there was no telling when she'd return back to North Carolina.

She hated to be alone the next day on Valentine's Day, but with a three day weekend to MSG, she'd land more suitors than needed. The brainstorming process began, as she gave both a hug and went to tell the guy she'd been luring that she had to take a rain-check on their spontaneous morning.

Sulaiman and Zohra thanked all their guests for coming and promised it wouldn't be the last gathering; they stayed until everyone had left the mansion and when the hired armed security personnel radioed in to Sulaiman that the grounds were cleared after walking the German Sheppard's around the perimeters, he and his wife retired to their sleeping-quarters.

As soon as Zohra hit the room, she'd vanished into her private bathroom for a quick shower. As much as she wanted to soak in her spacious tub, she couldn't wait another minute to be in the comforting arms of her loving husband.

She entered the bedroom to a husband who stood in only his briefs. The sight of him almost took her breath away. His chiseled body sculptured to perfection, manhood bulging from the grey fabric, flaunting his assets for her glazed eyes, but she had the same exact effect on her husband. The red-head bombshell was admired by countless men and had killer curves, no nip/tuck like most of her female friends. Always one to be self-conscious about her looks, Islam had shown her true beauty comes from deep inside.

She noticed the scarlet velvet Chaise decorated with flowers, an addition to the house, one she loved. The post-baby svelte figure was just perfect to him. Her wicked bright smile, long flowing tousled locks. The lingerie she wore left nothing for the imagination.

Immensely satisfied the two were now alone. He pulled her into his warm embrace. "I want to congratulate you on coming home and for making it through the worst mental experience a woman could ever endure. I'm so proud of you. I've always known you were strong, stronger than me in most ways, I've missed you so much." He kissed along her soft neck. "I've missed your smile, your beautiful eyes, that sexy laughter of yours, the way your soft diva fingers run through my hair, such a wonderful touch." He pecked her lips. "Your taste, Lord, I missed your taste. That scent of yours. I missed the femininity you possess, the conversation you bring and the realness you have, and having you around again will take everything to its rightful place. Your presence will balance things out, hand and glove."

"I love you so much, Sulaiman. It pained me so to be away from you. I promised not to ever withhold anything from you. I make no excuses for my horrible actions."

"Let's not travel back in time. All is forgiven, but I'll hold you to your word. I know that time changes a person's demeanor, the distance affects a person's feelings and the solitude does things to one's mindset. Through your previous letters, I got the sense that you still carry that abrasive attitude with you. Don't get me wrong, it's nothing we can't adjust and that attitude drew me to you to begin with, but know the road we journey on will have obstacles in it. Yes, we left the game alone, but we've created many enemies and I suspect they haven't forgotten or forgiven us just because we submitted to God," he said, unable to wait any longer for the two of them to submit to one other.

"Sulaiman, I thought about this many of nights. We have to clean up our messes in order to live the life we wish to have. More than anything, I need to know you have my back on this." She held her chin up to gaze into his eyes. "It's the only way. We'll never have the peace we so vehemently desire with drug lords seeking our blood."

Overwhelmed with the decision to do what's right verses allowing the past to come back and haunt them. Antonio's words echoed in her head, and as she vowed before, no one was going to harm her family.

The two made love until the dawn, showered than offered salat.

Chapter Six
Saturday, February 14, 2015

Sulaiman had been the perfect gentlemen from early that morning until they went to lunch. The women slept late, but had been awakened by a lavish hot breakfast in bed, freshly cut red roses and a box of imported dark Irish chocolate. He didn't celebrate holiday's, but knew most women took the special occasions to heart and rather the gift be large, small, expensive or a handmade card, it was the intention behind it.

Zohra had been engrossed deeply in prayer. Her Aunt Cassie had arrived and watched intently, furious her niece had dropped her faith and embraced the religion of Muhammad. After the completion of the salat, Zohra rose to the sight of her mother's sister's evil-eye.

"This Blackman has you beating your head on a carpet. I can't believe this is the life you chose over one of power and luxury. A Black man, Dee… what's gotten into you?"

"He's a human being."

"Humph. Whatever." She contorted her face in disgust.

"The man I married was created by the God we both worship and believe in." She didn't know why she felt the need to explain.

"They think they're better than us, boasting that they were created first. They who? The few with the same mind frame as the KKK! We can walk out that door," she pointed, "And ask the first 100 whites the same question and they'll say that whites are superior to everyone and whites were here first. Not to forget, that we've been enslaved to almost every known race to mankind."

"History isn't pretty, I'll admit. But, we can't change what happened. There are no different races in Islam; we are all brothers under one banner. An Arab is not superior to any foreigner, nor is a white man superior to the Black man. Every single one of us will in the end return to God. Islam means submission to the one God, the Lord and creator of the world. Muslims must keep this in mind at all times, God's oneness. See, God has ordained for the Muslims, certain acts of worship which are called the pillars of faith. Now, what you've witness me doing moments ago is called Salat, which is prayer in Islam. I've commanded to do so five times a day. It is said prayer washes the believing Muslim's soul from all evilness and makes the man complete and sincere in one's beliefs and faith. It also makes man totally aware of his Lord's might and power over all the worlds He was created. Once a Muslim submits, all obedience is to his Lord.

"All that sounds fine but why do you have your head covered, and do you support terrorism?"

"This is called a hijab. My veil isn't a symbol of some sort of oppression."

"Darling, the news doesn't lie. I see the killings every day! We all see the killings."

Zohra quoted a verse from her sacred book. "They try to put out the light of Allah with their mouths.

However the light of Allah will continue to glow even if the unbelievers hate it." She paused, still poised and calm. "I'm not saying everything the news say is a lie, yet it also promotes violence and takes things to extremes, but, Aunt Cassie, terrorism is a violent manifestation of extremist claiming to be Muslims, only seeking out to destroy our religion and those who don't support the evilness of the ills and their pathetic causes, and as the saying goes, *Islam is perfect, people are not.*"

"Okay, enough of the religion 101."

The two continued on. Cassie admitted she liked the hijab, the lovely colors. And understood that true beauty and purity lies within males or females, and that God isn't like man who looks upon your appearances, financial status, and number of children, but rather, He peers into the hearts of man and rewards and punishes man for his deeds. Cassie shook her head, who knew her niece was so deep and informative. The women spoke briefly about the future of the families' cartel. Cassie giving one last plea to no avail, then had Zohra walk her back to her waiting husband, who'd tried to drill Sulaiman but came out with much respect for the man.

Cassie's husband kept his thoughts to himself, helping his wife into her coat. She wondered what the book was he had tucked underneath his arm.

"Did everything go alright?" he questioned, noting a different look to his wife than before.

"Yes, I'm fine dear. I could've sworn she was preaching. She's changed, but, I do think it's for the best. Only time will tell. What about the husband, I've met him several times before, but to be honest and in all fairness, she has herself a jewel. I'm stuck in my old ways. You know how I was raised."

"My love, we know very good blacks, respectable, honest and hardworking, decent, church going folks."

Cassie promised to make some changes, starting with self.

"I talked to the husband, a very fine and intelligent man. To be perfectly honest, hands down the smartest I know. He assured me he wasn't with our niece for financial gain, showing me several lucrative business adventures before he met Dee," he said over the hood of the Bentley, as their driver helped her inside the expensive luxury car. "He also has the means to bring the war out of her and I saw it in his eyes, it won't be long. Sulaiman will trade in his rug to rule the empire, and when he does… were looking at a billion a year."

"Are you serious? Do you understand what you're saying?" Cassie's eyes lit up at the very thought of it all.

"I'm not kidding. He's that good and deadly. I saw murder written all over the guy's pupils. He's no petty hustler, nor is he some guy chasing tennis shoe money. He's the real deal."

"Let's pray what you say is true," she said, with erected nipples. "This indeed was a true turn-on."

He kissed his wife, noticing her berries. "Let's go home, so I can take care of that." He smiled, as they drive pulled off.

Zohra went upstairs to get dressed. Sulaiman had plans to take them shopping to some of New York's most expensive and luxurious shops and malls. The trio was going to catch eyes at tonight's event, and the day after at Sunday's All-Star game.

Both women were equally pampered and spoiled by Sulaiman. The black card he'd given them was told to be used without caution. Temptation couldn't believe how Sulaiman tossed money around as if it were mere paper of no value. This made her rethink the choices she made when searching for men, and it definitely pained her to know that Sulaiman had slipped through her clutches. Zohra was her BFF, yet somewhere deep in the core of her heart, she envied Zohra, and a streak of jealousy formed in her chest and grew by the moment, like a spreading cancer. She found herself brushing up against him every chance she got, playfully, with flirtatious comments, especially when the opportunity presented itself and Zohra wasn't around. She remembered how she flashed her clean shaven cunt to him at her uncle's house a while back and she'd never forget how his lingering eyes pierced its target while listening attentively to her uncle's words.

She knew at the time he wanted his hard cock inside of her, his bulge was evidence, but a poor choice on her behalf screwed things up by trying to look out for Zohra who didn't deserve a man of Sulaiman's status. Temptation planned to rectify her mistakes, a mistake found to be a regrettable one. The way he held the small of her back when he walked with the two made it much more complicated. Those strong hands were supposed to be on her body at night, holding her firmly, but no, something had to give. Zohra, true indeed was her girl, but she'd much rather have Sulaiman as her man.

Ayesha caught her peering through the door of Zohra's room while she was downstairs talking to her Aunt Cassie. Sulaiman had just gotten out of the shower and had been standing nude, drying off. Clueless as to what Sulaimn had been doing, Ayesha decided to ask him later without causing a scene.

Later that night, the trio had dinner, and then went back to the All-Star events, and just like the previous night, all three had a blast. But Sunday's All-Star night, Zohra couldn't return; her monthly had kicked her ass and cramps made it impossible, so she told her husband to enjoy himself and take Temptation with him so she could get some much needed rest, and Temp could hopefully meet a man.

The Garden was on fire. The two set on the row behind Mutumbo and Clinton watching LeBron put on a clinic. Westbrook made treys as if tossing the ball into the ocean. The two joked about Kevin Hart being crossed-over by the little league black female pitcher and his dance battle with Nick Canon. Afterwards, they headed back to the limo.

Sulaiman texted his wife a letter while on the way to an exclusive club:

Just wanted to brighten your night- you've definitely brightened so many of my days. When the Lord sends a special blessing, he often wraps it in the form of a very special person. Words can't adequately express how special you are as that blessing in my life. You are a gift, one that I'll always cherish- beautiful, caring, intelligent, loving and fun, bringing so much happiness to my world. Being close to you is a privilege and a joy. I'm so blessed to have you as my encourager and friend, and I fully understand the Lord poured out His blessings upon me when He brought you into my life. My treasure, I adore you. Your love deserves an encore.

He completed the text just as the limo pulled in front of the club. Guilt had consumed Sulaiman. He loved his wife immensely, but Temptation lived up to her name tonight, and not to mention, again, she wore no panties. He did all he could to prevent himself from taking a peek or two at the eye candy by lowering his gaze, but tonight, his iron-will had somewhat rusted. Tonight, Temptation wasn't as flirtatious which made him wonder. There was no loud cussing, outburst of laughter, or blatant disrespect, in fact, she was the perfect woman, and the fact that all eyes had been on her and she clung to him, made him think something was definitely wrong.

"Temptation, what's wrong? I've noticed you haven't been acting yourself," he questioned.

"I'm cool," she responded, taking sips of her drink with a small umbrella in it.

"I know you, you're not cool. That live, vibrant, sexy and confident beautiful woman isn't acting herself."

"That's just it, Sulaiman. You named everything but intelligent. My looks are all I have to offer to a man."

"This isn't true. Not many women attended medical school."

"Nor do many get kicked out for drug sellin'. I have no job, no money, or man. I survive from gifts men heap upon me."

"What is it that you wanted to do? I have four restaurants. Maybe you can help me out and manage them. Certainly you're great with figures."

"I don't know, Sulaiman. All I know is drugs."

"That's how Jay Z started, but look at him now. Utilize those skills, and never down yourself. I didn't have to mention intelligence. Had I not believed you were, you wouldn't be here tonight. Plus, it feels good to have a woman of your nature by my side. It felt good to have actors, comedians, entertainers and ball players envy me for one night, not to take away from my lovely wife, but you understand what I'm saying."

"Sulaiman, don't play me. I'm quite sure you've been in the company of many beautiful women."

"Yes, to be exact I have. But rarely do I have an opportunity to be in the company of someone like you. I can find a bus load of beautiful women, but most have self-esteem and self-worth issues. Mentally damaged or lack of the means to want to repair themselves, and not to mention, the ones who'll do anything to please you even if it ruins them. Naw, you can have that."

"I've been through a lot myself."

"That's it. You have, but you haven't allowed your adversities to overcome you. Now, are we going to continue to let the night pass on sob stories and what-ifs? Or dance the night away and enjoy ourselves? Your call," he held his hand out.

"Sulaiman, you never cease to amaze me."

"Hey, what can I say? I'm not your average guy." He hunched.

Temptation accepted his hand and the two danced the night away.

About an hour into the groove, bumping and grinding holding nothing back, she found herself to be no match for Sulaiman on the floor. She excused herself to use the restroom after slow dragging to a slew of oldies but goodies. Passing by a couple of Rude Boys who sat in the back on the club getting lifted and selling pills, it hit her. "That's it!" she murmured to herself. *The incident would be the start of her betrayal....*

Temptation could spot a deal 100 miles away in the dark. Boldly, she walked up to one of the dread lock ballers and asked if he had two Molly's and a killa blunt. The light traffic volume going to and fro from the restrooms were at a minimum, a relatively mild night, and with a careful glare from head-to-toe, to expedite any problems, one stood while the other held his hand out for the cash, in which she placed an old small-face hundred in his palm and then followed the guy who stood with his freshly twisted lions mane; he diddy-bopped with a natural gait to a more secluded area.

Temptation was given her requested product and some of Cali's finest bud. Indeed, this would not be a typical night.

When the dealer returned to his seat, he turned towards his partner. "She's grown and sexy."

"No, she's an insidious disease," he said, twisting a spiff. "Whoever encounters her tonight, will remain in her web, mercy me."

Temptation returned with drinks in hand, Sulaiman politely refused. "I don't drink alcohol."

"Neither do I, don't forget, I know what kind of business you own, a non-alcohol exotic restaurant."

He laughed heartedly, excepting the spiked mixed drink. He told her the limo driver said they were snowed in and it was impossible for them to make it back to the mansion since all the streets were covered in a quarter of an inch of black ice sheets, and the majority of the secondary roads were impossible to travel on. He informed her they would have to find the nearest hotel for the night until road conditions were feasible, and they'd return home as soon as the weather permitted.

Temptation thanked her lucky stars as he went on to say they would have to share a room since the hotel was booked to capacity. Jokingly, she told him no funny business, and the two walked out arm in arm, braving the cold New York winter, GMA had so vehemently warned them about.

The winter blast was colder than usual back home in her new place of residence, Henderson, which was 7 degrees for the highs, the wind chill factor made it feel more like 0 below.

Both high, after a block and a half walk, they were finally in the warm comfort of the hotel the driver had so kindly paid for, knowing it would come back to him two-fold. She had snuggled up closely to him during the entire walk. With each step he felt woozy, attributing it to the weather or lack of conditioning.

By the time they'd made it to the room, the pill was in full effect.

"Here, let me help you out of your clothes," Temptation said, with deviousness laced in her satin voice.

The drink he thought to be non-alcoholic and the now contact high from the weed had him feeling horny, as she turned up the music and asked him if he'd mind her getting out of her wet clothes.

"Sure, I don't want you to get sick," he slurred.

"Help me unzip this dress will you."

Somehow, he eagerly sprung to his wobbly feet, laughing at his silliness, and his hands touched her flesh, and his knuckles burned like hot coals in a fireplace on Christmas night in Michigan.

When the spaghetti-strapped dress fell to a heap on the floor, her nude body glistened in the lights, evident of a well-baby-oiled body, soft, and toned to perfection. He didn't know what happened after that, but he found himself kissing her succulent breasts, then he pushed her to the king-sized bed, stripped off his underwear, and within seconds, he was in between her thighs sucking the first of many orgasms out of her.

They were like two rabbits screwing, and she found herself in every position imaginable, and then some. Temptation let him do things no decent woman would allow, giving him free reign to do as he pleased, and the pleasure was well worth it.

The second pill was given as he took a break, sweating profusely as he gulped down room-temp bottled water. He was totally out of it, she was fully alert. After several hours of mind blowing sex and finally unable to take any more of his massive manhood, the two fell asleep naked, spooning one another, a night she'd never forget, one he'd have to keep secret for the rest of his life.

She took out her Smartphone and took a few selfies of them for insurance. One never knows when they might need to play a trump card.

Chapter Seven

Antonio got a call from his right-hand man, Benny Burnsville. One of the buyers had a problem with his shipment and he wanted to speak directly to him, 18 kilos wasn't small talk with a middle-man. Usually, Antonio spoke to no one but knew once the old Mexican drug lord was able to return home, this would be a valuable connect. His town was hot, and southern Mexico had been flooded with Mexican Navy Marines, and officers guarding an area where 43 teachers, college students were feared to be buried in mass graves.

The chronic drug violence had him on the run. A cycle of grotesque violence had marred Mexico, and operatives had leads he'd left Iguala for Manhattan, and was now planning to set up shop in one of New York's most lucrative cities.

Agents had notified the U.S. of Hector's whereabouts, implementing him in a string of kidnappings and extortions.

Unbeknownst to either men Hector's work was okay, but he felt like he should've been given a little more since this was his third purchase of 10 or more bricks. The two men talked at lengths, coming to an agreement, and as they shook hands, agents descended upon the two with guns and assault rifles trained on their targets.

Antonio was snatched out of his Mercedes-Benz and slammed ruthlessly onto the ground in his Nautica cable knit, 501 blue jeans, black leather Calvin Klein jacket, Ray-Bans and a scent of Issey Miyake along fear. The expensive necklace around his neck was buried in the snow from its weight and his time piece was proof of his lucrative drug selling life-style. He thought about running, as most drug dealers do, but decided against it; his pants sagged low and his shoes weren't tied tight enough to make a quick getaway in the snow. He should have listened to his mother and pulled them up, but it was too damn late now.

 Antonio was handcuffed from behind after being thoroughly searched, then shoved, roughly, into the back seat of a police car with all eyes focused on him.

 Benny couldn't describe how furious he was, helpless, unable to do anything but watch and be thankful he hadn't been included in the sweep.

 The F.B.I. concerned themselves more with Hector than Antonio. Hector had been on their radar and they received a tip from an informant inside of Hector's organization, who also supplied them with the reputed drug lord Antonio War. Because of this, they managed to hit two birds with one stone, and today was a major bust for the department.

 From a far, Benny watched his childhood friend/boss slump in his seat, and knew if Antonio didn't get out of this jam within 24 hours, a lot of people were going to suffer for it and he was very lucky he hadn't driven Antonio today as he usually would have. Antonio had his personal driver drive him while he trailed behind in a black SUV with three trained killers, all with enough weapons to receive a life-sentence each. He sat attentively, mentally recording everything, daring not to drive off.

One of the men gathered the weapons and chanced it by exiting the vehicle and walking down the sidewalk with a duffle bag that would hold numerous charges if nabbed. Once Joe bent the corner like the average Joe, Benny breathed normally, then extracted his Smartphone from his costume suit jacket and dialed his old boss's number. The two were close. He'd been in control of all the drugs stationed at a secret warehouse in the Bronx.

Antonio didn't have to wait a second, debating on who he'd give up to get himself out of this predicament. He knew he wasn't built for prison and definitely wasn't going to pretend to be. His pretty boy looks were guaranteed to have someone straddling his ass in a shared prison cell, perhaps a white biker or a big, black, ugly weight-lifter in a gang. He knew the name *'War'*, alone, would get him killed, for his family was responsible for at least 50 bodies at the bottom of the Hudson River.

Antonio began sweating profusely thinking about the several outstanding warrants that would pop up on the screen. Shit, he should have taken care of those long ago, but this was truly the end of him if he didn't cooperate. He knew the F.B.I. didn't want him; Feds always wanted bigger fish to fry. Dee Claire War would be the bass on the hook once he casted his rod into the detectives murky waters. His inexperience had finally caught up with him, and he was inwardly frustrated, upset with himself for breaking a golden rule to please a client when he had men who could've handled the situation. No one was to ever see his face or know of his drug ties, but he loved the attention it brought, the power, fame and sex, the life of luxury. But he also knew his cousin all too well, she rose to the wrath of her enemies and didn't take betrayal lightly, but this was a chance he had to take.

※※※

The twins played with their toys, one in a Fisher-Price Laugh & Learn Smart Stages Chair, the baby girl with kinky fire red hair like her mother couldn't be torn away from her Sesame street Let's Imagine Elmo. *They're growing too fast,* Zohra thought as she was handed her phone by Paris, her second call within 15 minutes.

The expression on Zohra's face wasn't a pleasant one. After a few shakes of the head, she knew her Aunt would be over shortly seeking assistance in the matter of Antonio. She hung up, vexed, fully aware of what Benny was hinting towards if Antonio didn't get out. She knew without a doubt he could be planning something twisted and devious.

Be-it she had changed, one could not forget she was still capable of being as demented as the next. *They have affected the streets with dishonor, he's no different,* she thought to herself before walking off. *How can I fight someone whose strength I know nothing of? Snitches have no hearts, and someone heartless is as dangerous as any walking killer, at least a killer may regret a kill.*

"Ayesha, I have to handle some very important business. Keep them business."

"That won't be a problem." Ayesha smiled, handing more toys to the toddlers.

"Where is my husband?" Zohra mumbled to herself, as she climbed the stairs. She had called him several times but received no answer, and she received the same response when she tried Temptation.

As she dialed her Aunt's number, the chimes sounded causing her to spin around mid-step, and Paris answered the door; it had to be Sulaiman or else security would have called first before allowing unwelcomed or unexpected guests to just pop in. But, the voice entering stopped her completely, she hung her head down.

She had to admit, her Aunt could run with most runway models. Her shape was fabulous for 51 and no cosmetic surgeries, at least none she knew of. Her mother, the oldest of nine siblings had been one of Bronx most radiant sort after women but he finally wooed her with charm and charisma.

Cassie Spicy Plum Lips went to talking as she thrust her $27,000 Salvatore Ferragamo Fiamma crocodile bag. Her Manolo Blahnik BB Pumps in Zebra Pony sounded throughout the mansion. "Don't just stand there, darling, come give your favorite Aunt a kiss."

Zohra took a deep breath, wondering how Cassie figured she was the favorite. When the two embraced, pressing La Prairie skin cheek to cheek, air kissing each side, Zohra inhaled the Baccarat Rouge 540 Limited Edition Eau de Perfume which came in a hand-carved Crystal Bottle with a price tag of $4,000 for her birthday.

"Dee, my son has been arrested. Please, see if you can get him an attorney. Apparently, he and his father ran their mouths a little too much. Williams's doctor turned out to be a fed who planted a bug in my husband's hearing-aid. Isn't that illegal?"

"Aunty, don't say another word."

"But….."

"Ssssshhh," she said firmly, holding her hand up to silence her.

Zohra took out her gold Apple iPhone and texted her Aunt in front of her. She read the message: do not say another word. You may be bugged as well. I'll have someone in here in just a few minutes to check you thoroughly. But, continue to act natural.

She made a call to Morgan who stopped what he was doing, tucked the Penthouse magazine away so no one would stumble across it, and rushed to the main house with his case. Morgan was a young Cohiba-smoking tech genius who loved professional poker, kept himself clean shaven, and dressed as if he knew Tom Ford personally.

Morgan hated to muddy his seven-hundred dollar Salvatore Ferragamo Leather sneakers in the snow, but duty called. He snatched his Tom Ford Suede bag with his equipment inside, reached for the Toshiba Chromebook 2 and slid it inside his black Christian Louboutin Alexis briefcase. He took another swig of scotch to knock the chill off and made his way over to the mansion.

With Morgan, it was always business. His homeboy had given him the job, one he happened to take seriously, and knew very well.

Paris let Morgan in. She liked him, wanted him so badly but refused to date someone she worked with, regardless of his pay or status. His cologne made her want to re-evaluate the decision.

"Good morning, my lovely Queen." Morgan removed his hat and gave Paris a million-dollar smile and hug.

"Hi Morgan," Paris tried to act professional. "Mrs. Cassie is in the living room."

Morgan peered into Paris's eyes, then nodded and followed behind closely, calculating each detail of her soft, jiggly ass as it bounced with each step. Her long, curly, brown, bouncy hair hung in big beautiful curls from having slept in rollers that were wrapped tightly in a silk scarf overnight. He wanted her like a sinner needing forgiveness, how long he'd be able to keep his composure remained to be seen. When Morgan's eyes met Cassie's he almost forgot about Paris, *men.*

Cassie stood up and observed the built Black man who was staggeringly beautiful, sending chills all over her. Maybe this was the reason her niece found herself with the forbidden fruit. She extended her well-manicured hand, and was shocked when he took it in his firm, yet gentle, grasp and lightly planted a kiss on her white knuckles, burning the flesh and sending an unfamiliar heat between her thighs, causing her cheeks to become flushed.

"Well, Mr. ……"

"Morgan. And may I ask who your lovely self may be?"

"Sophia War, everyone calls me Cassie."

"Sophia sounds much more sophisticated, royal and exotic."

Paris spun, her jealousy wouldn't allow her to witness anymore. Had she not been in the room, she would have bet the two would be on the couch fucking like young teenagers in heat.

"Mrs. Sophia."

"Please, only Sophia." She flirted dangerously, if only Zohra could see her now.

"Why, yes. Sophia, I'm going to have to ask you to do something you may not be comfortable doing, but it's very important that you understand if you don't cooperate, you could find yourself in a prison cell with women lusting after you. No disrespect, but you have such a smoking hot body, who could control themselves?"

Did he say hot body? She thought, questioning herself not concerned about the prison statement.

"Do whatever is needed. I don't want to end up like my husband and son, who are both as you stated, *in prison cells* as we speak."

"Well, let's get started. Do you wish to go somewhere a little more private? I'll need all of your clothes."

"All of them?"

"Yes, every single piece. That is, unless you…"

"No, let's get this over with."

"I promise. I won't bite."

"Don't speak too fast. Come, let's find a room."

The two found a nearby guestroom and without any more haste, Sophia began to strip off her clothing. Piece by piece, she handed him a garment until she stood in only a bra and panties. Not once did she cover herself. She stood proudly, knowing that she had such an effect on men half her age; it was evident by the increasingly growing bulge in his pants, as he waved a security wand over every item.

He picked up the shoes and the device went off. Morgan placed his finger to his lips as Zohra had done earlier. He went over the right shoe again and behold, he twisted the heel which unscrewed and found a bug was inside. He showed it to her, placed it on a dresser, and then waved the wand over her body, down her now trembling thighs, brushing his knuckles gently against her intimate parts.

Not once had she ever cheated on William, but it had been seven long years since they'd had intercourse, medications wouldn't even help his soft limp dick turn hard. He'd gone to specialists all over the world, and the outcome remained the same, a dud.

Morgan stood behind her, his breath warm on her back, his manhood pressed into her backside, as he slid the straps of her bra down slowly. She could have sworn his lips touched her flesh, but was she imagining things? As her large breasts spilled forth, the only person to see them as of late was her female doctor. Self-consciously, she broke the steel-will she had and covered them, not because she didn't want him to see them, but embarrassed because of the long protruding nipples, begging to be suckled.

Unbelievably, the bra had been rigged by transmitters as well. He showed her then searched in his bag, found a writing pad and pen, and wrote down on it: I need the name of the person who brought these items for you.

"My maid, Brianca, she's been with me about a year now. Very dependable, but she found herself in some trouble recently when the cops raided her apartment, searching for her boyfriend and found drugs in the home. Why? You don't think…"

"Not only are you beautiful, you appear to be rather intelligent enough to understand my logic and reasoning. So, I will not belittle your wisdom. I do think she's the one who's responsible," he said after placing the devices into a glass square container, and securing it so whoever had her wire-tapped lost connections. "She's the only one who would have close and personal space with you. Who else could have put them in a bra you wore and in the brand new, and might I add, beautiful heels? But, don't let her know that you've found her out, two can play that game. I'm going to give you something to plant on her so we can track her every movement."

"Sort of like Spy Games?" Sophia asked with excitement. Her breasts now swung freely and to his liking, as she thrusted her chest outwards.

"Yes, except you'll be the sexy, devious lady."

"Stop, you flatter me so!" She blushed.

"I only speak the truth."

"You know, I've never cheated on my husband."

"I knew we had something in common."

"I don't understand."

"I've never cheated on your husband either," he joked.

"Morgan, I want to sleep with you so badly it pains me."

Morgan spun Sophia around, slid her panties to the side, fumbled with his massive dick, and slowly entered his manhood inside her. Upon his entrance she not only gasped from its size, but she also gasped from the guilt and shame.

"Who said we would sleep together? Your tight cunt got me wide awake," he said, muffling her moans and pants with the now unwired expensive bra.

Chapter Eight

The noon sun greeted Sulaiman's naked body which was still intertwined with Temptation's, who also slept naked. "My God, what have I done?" he asked himself fully knowing the answer. His head throbbed, giving him an indication that he'd been drugged, but by whom? He couldn't believe Temptation would do such a thing and disrespect the sacred bond of her friendship with his wife.

With lightning speed, he searched for his clothing and his phone; uncharacteristically, it had been cut off and laid close by on the floor underneath his socks. Zohra had to be worried sick. How could he be so stupid? He couldn't keep it a secret, for he didn't know if Temptation wouldn't be consumed by guilt and spill the beans on him. He sure as hell wasn't about to get blackmailed by anyone. The logical thing to do was to call Zohra and explain what little he did remember and hope their love was strong enough to pull them through, really.

Sulaiman found his hands trembling; this was a low point for him. He dialed. She picked up, no greeting.

"Sulaiman, I've been trying to call you and Temp all day. Where are you?"

"I'm… I'm still at the hotel."

"The main roads are clear, do I need to send someone to come get you two?"

"Zohra, we need to talk. Slow down."

"Solaiman, what's wrong?"

"Zohra, I messed up."

"You messed up! What do you mean, you messed up?" she asked concerned.

"I, I slept with Temptation."

"You *what*?!"

"She, some…someone drugged me."

"I don't want to hear your pathetic lies! Where is she?"

"Zohra, we need to talk. I can explain."

"No! What you need to do is act like nothing has happened and you both bring your asses here! If you're here within an hour, you'll never see your kids again," she threatened, before killing the line.

Sulaiman knew he was up 'Shit Creek'. He shook Temptation awake and told her they had to leave, A.S.A.P. before Zohra got suspicious.

He wanted to snap on her but he didn't have proof she forced it. To be honest, he knew full well what he was doing but knew there had to have been an influence.

Temptation stirred She peered at Sulaiman as he called his driver to notify him he'd be down in five-minutes.

Neither said a word. The slow elevator ride was brutal on his mind, remnants of their sex scent was evident in the tight closed quarters. The two spilled from the steel-box, sluggishly, making their way to the limo.

Once inside, Temptation broke the silence. "Sulaiman, we need to talk."

"I think we've talked enough."

"Not talking isn't going to change what has happened between us."

"You're absolutely right, but there isn't anything to talk about. What's done is done, and you have to be smart enough to realize that nothing can ever become of this!"

"But it can." She placed her had on his. "I never had anyone do what you've done. If we can work together, I'm sure it can last forever. Please, try to understand. In my heart, I felt that you were supposed to be mine, not Dee's. I saw you first, she knew I wanted you and I knew you wanted me, maybe it was a physical attraction, but it was a start."

"So, I'm supposed to leave my wife and kids over what could have been? Don't take this personal, but no pussy walking on two feet is worth me abandoning my family."

"We can't run away from what we shared last night. I know magic when I see it. You weren't that high as to not know what you were doing. You willingly accepted that drink, *and* my body. That dick of yours had no problem standing erect like a prize winning Vizsla."

"I'm not going to entertain that. But, to drug me into bed with you, that, even that is a low for you, Temptation."

"Maybe so, but we both enjoyed ourselves tremendously."

"Whatever," he said, as the limo pulled up to the mansion's security gate.

"She doesn't have to know. This can remain our little secret and we can continue it as long as you wish. Put me in an uptown condo where I can be close to your side when you need me."

"Sadly, she already knows."

"Sulaiman, what do you mean?"

"Just as I said, now let's get this over with," he said, not waiting for the driver to open the door.

Temptation had to gather herself and brace for the unknown.

The driver opened the back door for her. The snow thick and heavy had shrouded the elegant grounds of the mansion, but someone had cleared a pathway for those seeking to return or leave the premises.

Zohra stood with her hands on her thick hips. She was so disgusted with Sulaiman and it pained her to even look at him.

"Look at you two, how dare you disrespect me in such a manner? Do you know who I am?! What I can do to the both of you!? In Charlotte, I sat by while you screwed female after female; sex with Sloane the physical therapist, and her friend Amber from Detroit, Dutchess, Tracy Dimes and her friend, you even had a threesome with Rita Jordon!"

"You've spied on me?"

"Damn right, I spied on you! I also kept the feds from snatching you from the streets."

"And *you*," she said, as her eyes shot imaginary daggers toward Temptation, "I let you in my home, around my husband, my children. Temp, how could you? I trusted you implicitly and this is how you repay me?"

Temptation had had just about enough and interrupted like Kanye, and took the stage. "You stole him from me! Sulaiman was supposed to be *my* husband, but no... at the airport in Charlotte you sunk your vampire teeth into his neck, greedily taking him from me, knowing I had feelings for him!"

"That's insane! Are you going to stand there and allow her to continue to speak such foolishness?" Zohra shouted. Her focus was now on her husband. "This was just another challenge to you! Okay, this discussion is over." She spun to leave from Temptation and her speechless husband's presence.

"Like hell it is!" Temptation snatched her arm.

"Don't you ever put your filthy hands on me again," Zohra flared up.

"Or what?" Temptation asked, closing the distance.

"Alright, Temp. That's enough." Sulaiman finally spoke, getting in between the two separating them.

"Don't touch me!" She slid out of Sulaiman's reach as if he was scum, disease.

Zohra peered sharply into Temptations eyes. "Get your belongings and get the hell out of my home before I have you tossed out. You are no longer welcome here."

"I need a ride."

"No, you need to get moving, don't test me."

Temptation stormed to the guestroom to collect her belongings. She was glad to get out of Zohra's home, and Sulaiman not defending his wife had given her hope. Zohra stood at the door watching her best friend struggle with the luggage, but dared not lift a single bag. Dragging the heavy luggage which had increased in size since her stay, she threw one down the stairs and then the other. She then told Zohra to throw them away like she was doing their friendship. She proceeded to leave the home with her head held up high, even with insults being hurled at her back.

Zohra grabbed the second luggage, and with sheer brute strength, she snatched it up without hitting a single step. As Temptation opened the door, Zohra slung the luggage out and slammed the door closed behind her once best friend with tears threatening to burst forth.

Sulaiman tried to comfort his wife and at the same time, opened the door and told Temptation to come back inside until the driver was ready to take her back to the hotel. This infuriated Zohra, instead of loving his wife, wrapping her in his embrace, this wasn't the homecoming she'd expected, and he was feeling sorry for his lover, her enemy.

"She's not going to use our driver. Sulaiman, listen to yourself."

"Zohra, listen to yourself. Taxis don't travel secondary roads because of the hazardous road conditions caused by the freezing weather."

"I don't care. I want her out now!" She stomped. "And you get your things and leave too since you want to play Russian roulette!"

She didn't want to appear overly optimistic, but she had to pour the gas on the flames. "Remember your own words bitch. You always keep an eye on the person who's closest, the one who has the most valuable information, the one with the most to gain," Temptation said in a devious tone.

"See what anarchy she causes? You know what, I'm not going to even stand here and clown myself. Take her wherever you want. I have other matters to deal with. I hope she was worth it." And with that, Zohra turned and left. Temptation's actions were inexcusable, inappropriate to say the least.

Sulaiman turned to leave. He knew he'd fouled up seriously, but at the same time, he wasn't cruel hearted where as to leave Temptation stranded in the cold where anything could happen to her. With keys in hand, he stomped out of the house and headed to the Range Rover.

"Come on," he said, snatching up each piece of luggage, kicks pounding the snow into slush, dutiful. Temptation followed closely behind.

The Range crept through the snow with ease. Sulaiman felt it was the most reliable vehicle for all purposes.

"Sulaiman, the hotel is booked. You'll have to take me somewhere else," Temptation said.

"We're going to my condo. You can stay there until I figure something out."

"What's there to figure out? I screwed up big time," she added somberly.

"*We* screwed up big time. I refused to allow my wife's anger to blame this totally on you. My actions were as contagion as anyone's."

This wasn't some insignificant matter to be swept under the rug. Its effect was surely to damage his integrity and reputation. In his wife's eyes, this was a grievous situation of magnitude, and the gravity, staggering, a foul taste of mischief, if you will. He knew it wasn't a good idea to intermingle with the opposite sex. He hadn't realized Temptation's ulterior motives, but thought he could ward off any such flirtatious attempts and clear assertion of infidelity. Now, by him being grossly disloyal to his marriage, he witnessed things quickly dissolving and thought it best to remain silent to keep from sticking his foot further in his mouth.

Sulaiman's Smartphone reacted, he pulled the phone from the console and peered at the screen, it was his financial advisor, McKenzie Love. "Sulaiman, sorry to bother you, but I need you to come down as soon as possible. Business, it's climbing rapidly here in Charlotte and we have a major deal to sign off on. The Greensboro meeting needs to have the CEO in attendance. We're about to build a thirty-two story hotel and High Point wants to furnish all rooms once we have the contract signed." McKenzie was so excited she was nearly out of breath.

He peeped over towards Temptation as she watched the video, *Thinking Out Loud,* on her phone; the dancing couple had her mesmerized.

Sulaiman turned his attention back to the conversation with his adviser who continued to ramble on. "McKenzie, I have a few things I seriously have to handle, to tie up here, and don't know how the airports are going to handle this weather situation, so let me get back to you shortly, and if a flight isn't on the agenda, I'll have to drive." He clicked off.

He informed Temptation that they were going to stay at the condo tonight, and if they couldn't get a flight out, they'd drive back to North Carolina. The two had been through a lot together, and deep inside, he knew she was right, had not Zohra come into the picture, things may have been different. Temptation had done so much for him in the past, there was no way he could forget her loyalty. She had introduced him to Birdie who not only helped him at the mall in Charlotte, he thought she'd died with her finger on the trigger along with Crack Baby and Roll, but she survived. Birdie was in Rome assisting his friend Dice.

Reason, back at the mansion and now a part of his staff, proved to be a valuable asset. Zohra was upset with the lack disbandment of his members from the Charlotte committee he'd put together, who had all totally left the game and now were legitimate businessmen and women.

"Sulaiman, where are we headed to?"

"At the moment, I want you to check to see if there are any available flights out to N.C. if not, we're going to have to get it in on the road."

"What about traffic conditions?"

"The worst is to the North of us. We should be able to make if from here," he said, parking in the deck.

Sulaiman pulled out his phone and made a call. "I'm on my way up. I have a surprise for you."

Temptation raised an eyebrow. *What did he mean by surprise and who was he speaking to?* Devil's advocate she thought.

Sulaiman sat the luggage down, pushed his key into the lock and looked toward an anxious Temptation, who found herself to be the one shocked, "Tracy Dimes, what are you doing here?" she asked, now the one surprised.

"Temptation, long-time no see. Come in," she said, and grabbed her old friend by the hand.

This was strange. Temptation had no clue as to where Tracy Dimes had disappeared to. Who would have thought she was in New York City with Sulaiman? Temptation wondered if Zohra knew about this. What was the two's relationship? He said they were going to his condo. So many questioned needed to be answered, and Tracy Dimes had the answers, but she needed to be alone with her to get them. Clearly, Tracy Dimes didn't know about the wrath she incurred from Zohra, however, she knew her plans were souring right before her very eyes.

Sulaiman said nothing as he placed the luggage down and headed straight to the bathroom. Before long, he was taking a hot shower and ready to go see his nephew, and give Jamal's widow some money before he hit the road.

His sister-in-law had become a prominent doctor in New York, but he still felt obligated to make sure she had everything she needed to raise her son.

Tracy Dimes sat cross-legged on the sectional, rubbing the head of one of the two red-nose pit puppies flanking her, while playing with the other's belly. The two traded light chatter back and forth about Charlotte and those they knew and lost. Many who were still living were thrown into prison in herds; indictments passed out like government vouchers to suspects for the alleged crimes of racketeering, trafficking cocaine, heroin, firearms and conspiracy to commit murder, all gun-by-felony charges. The FBI and CMPD targeted west Charlotte, which was crime and gang infested, and also where most of the drug running and weapons were said to be found.

Sulaiman returned from the bedroom freshly dressed, so to answer one of her questions, it was evident he'd stayed there from time to time. His black hoodie from The Hoodie Shop in New York matched his all black gear. The puppies tore from Tracy Dime's lap over to their master, who would thoroughly have them trained as killers within months.

He asked Temptation about the flights and she said they were cancelled until further dates; so much for him attending the ceremony for Malcolm X in Harlem at the Malcolm X & Dr. Betty Shabazz Memorial and Educational Center. The Muslim leader was assassinated on Feb. 21, 1965 and he wanted to take his dad to the event.

"Ladies, I'll be back shortly. I need to make a run."

The girls nodded, and then Temptation went to her questioning.

Chapter Nine

Zohra hated to illustrate her position towards her husband and Temptation, but this spiritual bankruptcy had been his fault. The grievous nature of the crime pained her so, knowing the book of God gave stern warning on punishment and warnings against any leniency in enforcing the laws on adultery, and offenders were to be punished severely. He admitted to it and the unchallengeable evidence of the pungent sex scent left nothing to the imagination. There were no false accusations. Cheating had been agreed to be strictly restricted from. Yes, she had once told him it would be such a great turn-on to see another woman perform on him while she sat watching the show but this was before she'd gotten closer to her Lord.

She knew the social hygiene of her friend had been dumpster juice for years, but she also knew Temptation would never cross the relationship line. But, she refused to allow adversity to destroy her or undermine her vision for the family, which is why she called her husband and summoned him back to the mansion. Temptation superciliousness caused her to react in a hauteur fashion, even though she'd known better, especially since Temptation was an insidious disease.

So much for a typical day, she thought, as she sat sipping on green herbal tea. Ayesha had taken the kids out because Zohra didn't want them seeing her acting as she had acted earlier. It shamed her more than anything to allow them to see her rant off at their father.

At first sight of Sulaiman, she wanted to cry. How could he have let this happen to them? But she didn't bring him home so he could face more harsh criticism. The way he'd stolen her heart was criminal and she wouldn't let it go that easy. He noticed a book to the side of her, the title, *"Why Do You Let Him?"* and wondered what it was all about.

Zohra reached for the remote and turned down the radio. Earlier, while reading the well-written book, she'd rocked-out to the sounds of *"I bet my life"*.

The world suffered enough with moral and social degeneration, to her, the incident was totally awful, a heinous crime, an acknowledged abomination which stained his character in her sight. There was no way she'd allow this to ruin the peaceful harmony of their happy home. The children were innocent in this ungodly situation, and she refused to expose them to his adultery and deprive them of a life with both parents, making her a single soccer mom. Their lives didn't deserve to be miserable. Eventually, she'd forgive him, but for now she had to remain staunch on her previous decision just to keep them together, but for now, that would be all, a fly in an ointment situation.

"Zohra, I...." Sulaiman started to say.

She held up a hand. "Please, Sulaiman. Allow me to speak first. You've had your chance."

"I didn't come to argue. If anything, I'll clean out my belonging and be gone. Call your attorneys and whatever you want, it's yours. I won't fight it."

She said nothing at first, and then a lightbulb went off. "You know and understand that modesty is just as important to the man essential, as it is to the female who practices the faith." Zohra stood inches away, but kept direct eye contact as she expressed herself. "Preventive actions of some sort must be made by you when dealing with women who have ties with us. I expect you to guard yourself at all cost… these are my private parts," she said, as she now inched closer to him, planting her nose to his, thus squeezing a hand full of meat to emphasize her point. "Our children will not suffer because of this."

"I love my kids and I'll never hurt them. I'm not some dead beat dad."

"That's what you told me, Sulaiman. That you loved me and you'd never hurt me. I know you're not a deadbeat, but you texted me words of love before you had sex with her. So, excuse me if I'm hurt." She spilled into his arms crying. "Anyone but her, Sulaiman, ANYONE!" she cried out, pounding his chest in pain.

Sulaiman allowed his wife to pour forth her justified anger. It crushed him to see her sob so. He knew she had a pretty rough time comprehending the betrayal, so many had died at her hands for less, yet, she struggled inside for the unity of her family and the love she had for him, a mental battle, one in which would carry scars for years to come. He was her first, so he couldn't imagine allowing another to touch her body sexually. He hoped their shared enthusiasm for one another and their love and faith in which brought them together to begin with was strong enough to will her to fight for one another.

Under the crystal chandelier they kissed, all wasn't lost but nothing wasn't forgotten either.

Sulaiman hated to deliver such unexpected news so suddenly. "I have to go out of town. My team is in a major deal and one appears to be pretty solid. A hotel with investors and a furniture factory wants the contract to supply the entire building."

Zohra said nothing, her thoughts mute. She decided it was a need, she had money saved, so did he, but until their enemies were no more, they needed the capital, and it was necessary to turn every stone. "Is she gone?" she asked, referring to Temptation.

"No, she's with Tracy Dimes, the flight…"

"Make sure you take her home." Zohra knew in her heart this mistake would never happen again. He'd forever remain on point with all females.

"I will, and as soon as I get into N.C. I'll call."

"Do not let her poison you."

"She's a nuisance, but I can handle her. I might have erred once, but I plan not to make that same mistake twice, plus there won't be any drinking or clubs."

"Okay, Sulaiman… you can blame it on the alcohol all you want this time, but it better not happen again. I'm warning you." She smiled, yet he fully understood what she was hinting towards.

The two made their way upstairs so he could pack. Shocked his things were still intact his mind was a total wreck.

Zohra's phone chirped and she excused herself to answer it in privacy, although they held no secrets. It was her uncle. He ran the entire district and the number was the emergency line. Antonio had snitched, why was she not surprised? She gathered the necessary information, set up a meeting, and returned to her husband.

Sulaiman held his wife in his embrace, as he explained everything to her that had transpired the night with Temptation. She knew the powerful lure Temptation had, especially her being sober and Sulaiman drugged. She forgave him, and as he packed to leave, she wished they could share a special moment together. Most women would think her to be insane, but love conquered all.

She helped him pack his things. Occasionally, their hands brushed against each other's, sparks between the two were too strong to let anything rive their love. Yes, the two had rhubarb. It had to be known where she stood, but what a difference three hours of prayer would make, far from the reverie state she'd previously been engulfed in.

Zohra bent to grab his favorite pair of jeans from the bottom draw, and Sulaiman placed his palms upon her up-turned ass. "My eyes have never beheld such a glorious symmetry of the female anatomy until I laid eyes upon the sight of a goddess bending over."

Zohra peered over her shoulder. His magnetic words and hands began to hypnotize her.

The upside down heart could've only been painted by the most artistically artist, and still do injustice to the voluptuous body, each curve an extreme delight to his soul. He'd seen her dazzling beauty countless times before, but the God who fashioned such human should be praised for all of eternity. One could only imagine the softness of his stunning wife, to even visualize or dream of molding that form like a potter.

Sulaiman, slowly searching for wordless approval, slid her spandex pants down, revealing the sexiest, hottest ass ever. How could he have been so foolish to even think of touching another woman? The whiff of her fragrance as she spread her intimate parts for him to do as he pleased, mesmerized by the movement of his probing fingers pulling out to taste the nectar which would make the purest of honey jealous. He kept his gaze on the skin so lovely, fumbling with his distraction of a zipper, before bringing out his hardness in which he'd push inside the dewy slit. An hour later both found themselves showering off, revelry a fresh start.

Zohra walked her husband to the car. Had her Aunt knew the situation and vagary, she'd blow a gasket, but this wasn't about anyone but them, and her valiance attitude helped.

She went back inside. She had so much to deal with, for one, the Antonio situation. Sulaiman gave good advice and she hated he'd be out of town for a week or so, but she could handle it. Her mother schooled her relentlessly on these matters. She got dressed to meet a few people, her first stop LT. Wafer.

❦

Forty-five minutes later, she sat inside a diner across from the man who would bring her family information on every informant who wrote statements against the war cartel.

Lt. Wafer had a stack of papers in a manila file and slid it over to her, as he'd done so many times in the past. He then waited patiently for her to slide an envelope of her own over to him, but things had changed since the last time they'd met.

The last time Zohra sat in the diner was the day she killed Manny Gilinoski from Manhattan. Manny would oversee shipments of heroin from New England, in-turn, threatening to overtake her cartel.

It didn't take long to round-up the loyal men and women who anxiously and eagerly waited to get back on board. Many had heard about her marriage and the faith conversion, which for some, added to the speculation of her retrogress, but others who knew her well refused to repudiate, for anyone truly close to her knew she was more than capable of carrying out her work efficiently and effortlessly.

Zohra's credibility came from being one of Bronx's fiercest, drug lord's daughter, and the respected title had been earned, not given. The game had been taught to her thoroughly, broken down to the very last element, taking cue from the best in the business which put her in a league of her own. But the remarks weren't unraveling, in fact, as always she rose to such babbling and sort to drive any threatening cartels from the streets, even if she had to leave them strewn with dead bodies, leaving a void for the young up and coming.

This time, the envelope was given to him by a hulking character with bowling ball-sized biceps, grapefruit traps and a thick chest he could lose a golf ball in should he squeeze it together. The freak of nature was found in a small town called Warren, North Carolina. *Mountain*, Zohra's nickname for him walked over to the table and reached into his black M.J. suit and pulled out the familiar envelope he so vehemently waited for. Lt. Wafer had a hectic schedule, plus he didn't want to get filmed frequenting a mobster's establishment. So, he swiftly tucked his rat money away in his plaid coat, gave Kong a folder in return, with addresses and names to potential and current threats she should be very much concerned with. Then, he egressed without looking back.

Zohra had to move with strict caution. No margin for errors. Once she started the process there was no turning around. The files were more shocking than expected. The police reports stated various gang members were recruited by a raising drug network by the name of *Sons of the Boss*. The faction spent ridiculous amounts of money to hang anyone willing to make serious cash, regardless of their proclaim profession, there was room at the table for everyone, and all could contribute in some shape or form.

As the ranks increased in foot soldiers, more individuals were caught doing petty crimes not associated with the network and the 'Help Yourself Program' which stayed in full throttle began to come alive stronger than ever.

Dee Claire War's name continued to resurface. Ten-grand was placed on her head, 10 stacks to blow, eatin'-money in the street, for those hungry block huggers. They wanted her dead, a revenge killing for a missing body a little over a year ago. Zohra was supposedly the last one to see the third in command along with his men, who had all been sent to the diner by Eugene 'The Ghost' Slovanii.

Zohra called Sulaiman, and found out who had tipped off the feds. Her whereabouts were made known by an anonymous tip, right before they had boarded the flight to Russia. An evil smirk lifted her devious lip; it was time to pay the Bishop a visit, see if he wanted to make a confession.

Chapter Ten

Zohra called her husband to notify him of her intentions to see Antonio. He warned her not to pry too deeply in the case, for Antonio's dilemma was swarmed by the feds. Previously at the house she'd told him about her reliable sources at the NYPD who had called shortly after Antonio's arrest. Her uncle wanted her to come downtown, willingly, so she wouldn't be apprehended somewhere caught off guard. But, they had nothing on her, she wasn't squeaky clean but she'd made sure all her tracks had been swept away.

Sulaiman pleaded with her to lay low until her return, but she'd met with her staff. With drawn up plans and repeatedly going over the files by Lt. Wafer, there wasn't any more time to waste on prolonging to go after those who sort harm to her well-being by dealing a crippling blow to the network of so-called killers belonging to the New England based cartel who tried to manhandle its way into New York's drug scene. Not on her watch.

Now, the fight had to be made fiercely to prevent others from getting the same exact idea. With everyone on her team prepared and ready to strike, knowing their respective roles, the well-orchestrated strategy would be executed precisely as planned, deadly and swift, the norm.

Zohra was well-aware that she could have eyes on her, that's why she employed underpaid feds, everyone had a price.

This was very personal, a volatile problem which wouldn't be settled until everyone was dead. Zohra and her family could never have peace in their lives to raise the kids or serve the Lord.

With one last look at the list of names, one in particular struck a cord and he was about to be paid a visit.

She stood, stretching her weary bones and her coat was given to her. She held out both arms like the statue in Brazil, and in deed, she felt that tall.

She thought about her husband's words and wondered if he needed her in some way. She could only image what his ears had to endure while travelling back down south with Temptation. She handed her right-hand man the files and he vanished into the kitchen, set the papers on fire and watched as it burned to ashes before rejoining the ranks.

Knowing Sulaiman loved her reinforced her commitment and sincerity. The decision to serve her Lord wholeheartedly verses honoring her beloved husband for better or worst was indeed a tug of war.

Concluding the meeting, everyone knew their respective roles of the well-orchestrated strategy. The team filed out one-by-one, and after her bodyguards made sure all was clear, Zohra made her exit as the men scanned the perimeter.

She stood outside peering at the slip of paper she'd scribbled on, small enough to chew and swallow, quickly, in case the cops rolled up on her suddenly. Another paper she glanced at momentarily then walked to the black

SUV. The door was held open by a trusted friend, Nicolae, who assisted her inside the warm ride with her favorite kill-music on.

Nicolae peered around a last time, ensuring everyone's safety, and making sure no one was camping on roof tops with digital lens cameras and high powered scopes. He slid into the snug seat and let the warmth embrace him from the cold weather he'd stood in, which was his duty. Then, he nodded to Lance who drove the black SUV in the back, then to Bruce in the black bulletproof Suburban in front. Their driver pulled off; the first stop, a visit to see a bishop at one of the well-known Cathedrals.

The hits begin. The bodies mounted up.

Zohra hadn't been here in two years, but she knew the place well. Her mother would take her to the Cathedral and leave her amongst friends in the nave, while she attended to affairs of political domination and economical exploitations. Now the place was empty, but after descending from his throne a lone-figure stood close to the alter.

"I've been waiting for you." The short, Italian with worried green-eyes spoke softly.

From what he gathered, she had incredible resolve.

"Well then, this shouldn't take long," Zohra stated firmly.

The bishop knew of her mother's temper, if she held an inkling of that DNA, his time on earth would come to an end.

"How did you find out?"

"Does it matter?"

"I'm afraid not, but in all fairness, I truly cared for your mother."

"Oh really, is that why you had her riddled in the streets?"

"If you had stayed, they would've killed us all, one by one." His respiratory became jagged.

"Please, get it over with. I'm not afraid to die. I've made peace."

His lips mounted, there wasn't a day that went by that his actions hadn't haunted him. He made a regrettable error, became vulnerable under the pressure of the other cartels and mafia to make the call on the female who not only inherited a lucrative business, but abandoned it for a Black man and an imposing religion. This was a slap in the face to them all and she had to be dealt with as well, but he peered at his blood-stained hands moments before she had entered and made the discussion to get missing before the week was out, but it was a little too late and suddenly, he didn't feel so well.

"You don't have to be afraid to die. Many brave people die in combat, in systematic assassinations or unexpectedly. But you, there will be no peace, only suffering of the worst kind and we can do it here, or you can be a man and face the consequences of your fate."

He held his head up with the remaining dignity he had left, deciding not to go clawing and scratching draperies, furniture and carpet. The bishop followed closely behind, hoping his prayers would somehow be answered speedily.

That was one off the list, which was fairly easier than thought, and now there were three left to go.

Bishop Gills was swiftly whisked into the white van, head covered up, after his mouth and hands were duct-taped. He was driven to an unincorporated area in the south of the Bronx. Beads of sweat rolled from his forehead. The fierce bodyguards had been no short of rough with him, manhandling him throughout the excursion to an undisclosed abandoned building. He had that gut feeling, one gets when they know it's over, and he knew this wasn't going to be the peaceful death he'd asked for, so much for faith.

The short white-haired man thought about his beautiful petite wife again, and the thought saddened him. She'd never find out about his double-life, and then there was the possibility of never finding his remains. The more he pondered his sealed fate, the more he began to go into violent shivers, trembling uncontrollably. His stridulous cries reverberated against his mouth, as the van seem to drive for eternity.

The next stop, Brooklyn…

The sound of a television could be heard from behind the door. Zohra was fully alert to the moans and pants of the couple lying in bed making out. The second victim on the list wasn't with his epicurean wife, for she knew the brown-haired petite woman from the ballroom dances. Her flirty husband with a strong drink in hand, casually bantering amongst the rich and powerful, was dressed in costume-made attire, while the women, spoiled divas or whatever title one wished to label them, graced themselves in elegant fur hats, wraps and matching coats. But tonight, the young blonde picked the wrong night to get screwed, *literally*. Zohra screwed on the silencer with her black-gloved hand and aimed at her target with a calm professionalism that was haunting.

Thomas 'Feel Good' McGormick, thrust vigorously into the hot wetness unaware of his plight. Any split second, his lava would erupt and he was just seconds away from being sent to hell by the same female he doubted and maliciously spread rumors of her in capabilities, yet underestimating her means to show such drastic measure of performing her cartel duties as her counterparts would.

Now, quietly launching one of the deadliest mob hits the streets of New York would ever witness, she couldn't wait to see the pandemonium her vile actions would cause when key figures turned up missing and no one would know of their whereabouts.

Her rapid calculation of a speedy escape route made the job feasible, as she planned to get in and out, wasting no time. Unlike Gills, who she wanted crushed and broken, McGormick wouldn't suffer nor would the companion of his. She had more bodies to tend to, not including the remaining two on the list.

The tall, handsome, dark-haired man with the perfect hue of olive gripped the mattress as the orgasm ripped from his gut. The young, white female rode him reverse cowgirl, paying more attention to her clit and the long veiny member jackhammering into her, eyeing the motion from the shimmering light of the T.V. She squeezed her breasts, letting out a cry of ecstasy as a power voltage hit her in perfect timing, as the bullet from the magnum struck, widening her eyes in horror as her body twitched in spasms.

The dead body slumped over, catching 'Feel Good' off-guard. He thought the blond had been in the process of switching positions but saw his killer dressed in assassin black with the matching head gear. Daringly, he attempted to reach for his Ruger, but was stopped short with two slugs to the chest and gut, dropping his weapon to the floor. Her men scooped both bodies up and tied them down with iron-chains and steel weights, which would keep them at the bottom of the river. Cement blocks had a tendency of weakening, floating back to the top or drifting down stream, in which case, neither was good for business.

Zohra did all the hits by her lonesome; the only help provided was the removal of the corps. She wanted to make a bold statement, testing herself in varying situations and conditions as taught by her mother. She wasn't back in the game, yet a temporal leader, nevertheless, as deadly as they come.

This was the third attack in the week, and no one knew of the rampage she went on. Blindsided, not giving the mischief-mongers a chance to implore forgiveness. Her only mission was to uproot any future threat. The last of the two on the list, the trigger men hired to do the drive-by.

Black Unique and Raymond Red sat on opposite sofas, each with a female getting mind blowing head, smoking blunts, tripping off of *'The Devil went down to Georgia'*. The old school throw-back was way before their time, a classic Raymond Red found in his father's crates.

Nicolae and Bruce sat in the idling Cadillac Escalade beating their brains out, wondering what their boss' next move would be. Marcus sat quietly in the passenger's seat thinking she'd lost her senses, as her thoughts drifted to the last phone call from her mother, the saddest moment in her life. The former Marine Corps, anti-terrorist specialist, felt more comfortable behind the wheel, but she insisted that she'd drive and had everything mapped out. He rubbed his fingers through his slicked-back, oiled, black hair and embraced himself as the heel of her pink suede Louboutin pumps footed the gas, pink heels on a hit…who does that?

Zohra had been as unpredictable as the Carolina weather in February. Her unspoken words left them guessing and anxious to see another glimpse of her work. She navigated the vehicle which had been lined up directly with the living room. The rousing sound of Jeezy flowed through the old school BOSE speakers of the stolen vehicle, as he rapped about his pursuit of luxury from lucrative drug sells and street life.

The men inside were unaware, just as the others before them had been. This group was on the way to a graveyard in the next state over; burial land in New York was getting harder and harder to possess as the years went by. Six-foot holes were already prepared for the two men and their guests. She was emotionally drained, though not because she missed her children who were out with Ayesha and Paris, and her husband who was somewhere in Greensboro, N.C. conducting business, but she hated the fact that innocent women were caught with the men who had all become causalities of war.

Raymond Red heard the sound of a car tire peeling, and instincts made him jump up, peer out of the jalousie, and eye the unknown vehicle headed straight towards the house. Unfortunately, before he had the chance to jump or warn Black Unique, the old Brougham came crashing through the small apartment window, killing him instantly, and seriously injuring the others inside. The few remaining were snatched up violently, thrown into another Escalade and driven off.

The streets stayed bewildered. The hits continued in rapid sessions throughout the week. After a three week blood-bath, she claimed responsibility for the direct hits. She accelerated efforts, managing to evade another life-threatening situation when crews began to strike back, but the understaffed, untrained and ill-equipped men stood no chance, dropping like leaves in fall.

Zohra sat in Brianca Blair's office, the tough-as-nails detective was a no non-sense pit bull in Louboutins.

"Ms. War…."

"I've told you several times, Detective Blair. War is my maiden-name. The streets know nothing of me. I'm a very private woman." Zohra wondered how someone so lovely could be in law enforcement.

The brash intimidation fell upon deaf ears.

Captain Mount Wright entered the cramped office, peered at Zohra who he knew all too well. "Detective Blair, don't let her beauty fool you. She's a walking time bomb, ready to explode at any given moment."

"So, she's dynamite?"

"Worse! But Zohra, just like your mother, God rest her soul, you look spectacular!"

"Thank you, Captain," she said to her father's half son.

Captain Wright gave his Lt. the hit list to give Zohra, unbeknownst to Detective Blair. He also sent word that Antonio had given up an organization of Russian wise guys, and a bust where they had secret money drops that netted a quart of a million in pills and over 3.1 million in dirty money, pissing off the wrong guys who thought he worked for her.

Blair wondered why the Captain took so much interest in Zohra but learned the two were related, killing all speculations.

He sipped his iced coffee, as he watched Blair's face scrunch up, upset because she wanted to question Zohra more.

"Did you just shit on yourself, Ms. Blair?"

"Pardon me, sir?"

"I asked if you shitted on yourself?"

Confused, she sat puzzled at the question. "No, Sir."

"Well, stop sitting there mean-mugging Ms. Zohra and get to work. She's here to bond someone out, not answer a bunch of questions, there are killers out there ruining my city."

Blair said nothing, she knew a killer when she saw one, and Zohra was definitely *one*. Blair found what she was doing to be unnatural. She had watched the video, which depicted Zohra entering the Cathedral, then minutes later, two men in all black, wearing masks, came in walking Bishop Gills out at gun point.

The gruesome scene of him being murdered on the news station was like an uncontrollable blaze in a dry brush. Bishop Gills' dismembered body was chopped into small pieces. The only recognizable feature had been his head, which had been set in a black duffle bag and placed on the steps of the courthouse as a statement, with a note attached: *I'm coming.*

Security cameras were only able to get a brief silhouette of a black masked figure. Officials argued over the form of the lone-wolf who left the package to be discovered, adding fuel to the frustration of the teams of agencies working together to find out who was responsible for such despicable actions.

CSI and homicide detectives, side by side in their investigations, obsessed over being the first to crack the case. The Mayor blew smoke up the Captain's ass wanting those responsible brought to justice, his brother's daughter proceeded to be too organized for even his elect men. He thought back to the years he'd taught her how to shoot and use various weapons. He knew she'd rubbed noses with the wrong people in the drug spectrum, but the pugnacious leader she was groomed to be, now changed the way cartels thought moved and operated.

Zohra tried to keep death of the innocent to a minimum, plotting attacks against her targets, deploying car bombs which rocked buildings, flipping over vehicles, the likes only seen in Iraq. Camouflaged killers tote assault weapons, with police escorts to their destinations.

Those who sort her whereabouts gnashed and gritted their teeth in rage. The F.B.I. leads ended up useless, their disgust at piercing it together, plainly evident.

Her men labored on, more determined than ever to rid the streets of so-called snitches portraying to be gangsta's. Young and ruthless, yet educated and trustworthy, filled her ranks as it should be. Supplied by Sulaiman from North Carolina, he distinctively understood her request for loyalty.

There was an evident sadness that Sulaiman wasn't by her side; she loved his charisma, everything reminded her of him, even the antique decorating he added to the mansion. Those outside her circle, thought the love to be counterfeit, but she hadn't felt the need to prove anything. How could she compete with the many obstacles vying for his attention? Late last night they chat briefly while she loaded a clip to insert into a Tec 9, fat bullets and big holes? Their love was stronger than ever, and one and a million.

She walked past detective Blair leaning up against her black Corvette Stingray, absorbed in her thoughts, strategizing her next move. The much needed smoke break gave her time to focus, and the way the Captain rushed her out didn't sit well with her. It was time to do some serious digging.

"You shouldn't be smoking. It's harmful to your health."

"Killing is dangerous to your freedom," she bit sarcastically.

"Many kill, so we can cherish our sinful freedom," Zohra retorted.

To cause family riffs, the detective tossed out that Antonio had told her some pretty disturbing things about her. "Zohra el Djemal."

"Finally got the name right, huh?"

"Practice makes perfect." She smiled weakly. "What puzzles me is…why commence the killings now? Are you seeking power? I did a thorough background check on you and it turns out that you're squeaky clean. A newlywed, a first time mother… I just don't get it." She flicked the cigarette to the ground.

"Cops, one minute you're killing a man for selling singles, and the next you break the law by littering, and you're pointing fingers?"

"What about your faith? Isn't this giving it a bad name?"

"Beware! Truly, they are the evil-doers and evil-doers must be cut at the root Ms. Blair."

"Is that Qu'ran?"

"No, that's me quoting the truth. Good day, Ms. Blair."

Blair decried truthfulness in her words, but knew Zohra held a diabolical heart in her chest, but why all the killings? Soon she'd slip, they always did. The lady walking away in a pair of $2800.00 dollar heels, terrorized with deadly ambushes. Blair knew that even the best had bones to be dug up.

"Bzzzz..."

She extracted her Smartphone from her coat pocket. The sight of the caller's ID made a warm tingle in intimate places stir. Quickly, she spoke into the device like the quivery love sick fool she was, unconscious of the drones above head snapping photos of her.

The only thing on detective Blair's mind was her handsome thuggish lover who'd put her through school from his illegal gains, and hipped her to the street's pros and cons. He became the void no other man could fill. The thought of him walking around the house in his sagging bleached Levis, his Tommy Hilfiger Boxers and the scent of his lingering *GUCCI 'Made for Measure'* glued to her hickeyed neck welted from his tender lips….. She had covered the passion marks earlier that morning but just thinking about the things he'd done to her the night before caused her palms to sweat as she perspire between her cleavage. An animal… Mesmerizing… he was *all that*.

Brianca suddenly felt the need to get out of the coal-black expensive power suit Stephen had last bought her. She wanted to quickly change into her Victoria Secret set and dash back into his arms.

"Stephen! What a pleasant surprise. You miss me already?" Brianca purred into the phone.

"Bri," Stephen cried into the receiver, as a vicious blow to the gut doubled him over, "they're gonna kill me!" he said, spitting up blood.

The phone was ruthlessly snatched from his hand, and then the tall muscle bound Nicolae threatened him to remain quiet. At first, Brianca thought it to be some sick and cruel joke played by her prankster boyfriend, that is, until a speaker came into view on the screen.

"You're going to learn not to stick your nose into other people's business. Turn in your badge within the next hour or you'll lose one of these men."

The video-footage had been shot at her house. She could tell by the photo of her and Stephen taken on Christmas, downtown New York in front of the city's tallest decorated fern tree. Then the screen switched, and her father and stepmother came into view, tied and beaten unmercifully, faced down with guns to the back of their heads.

"Show me your face, you cowards!!!!"

This stirred a deep chord within her soul, as tears threatened to spill forth. A gut feeling told her, this would be the last time she'd see her beloved ones alive.

"You have three seconds to make a decision on which love ones live, your father or boyfriend... you don't choose, we kill both. One ... Two... Three! Times up, Ms. Blair, which is it?"

"My boyfriend!" she screamed into the Smartphone, and then watched three masked men with brass-knuckles disfigure him right before her eyes; with every hit something appeared to break.

Brianca fumbled with her keys and without any regard whatsoever for the law, found herself trudging the streets, weaving in and out of traffic, as she summoned the police to her house with the department issued phone she had on the dash board. As she drove recklessly, every few seconds she'd glance at her own personal phone which lay in the passenger's seat.

When Brianca walked inside the house, she ran over to her bloody boyfriend. He was still alive but life slipped away by the seconds as the angel of death hovered above his body.

"I'm here baby," Brianca cried, "don't leave me, damnit!"

She wondered why it was taking the ambulance so long to get there. Brianca cradled Stephen in her arms, tears dripping to his swollen lips, washing the blood down his broken chin.

He took his last breath in her arms, and she gave out a cry no lover should ever give. As she pounded on his chest, pleaded for him to hold on and not leave her like this, the cops came in with weapons drawn.

Someone had called the cops and reported seeing a woman assaulting a man; the caller also said the woman had a gun.

"I'm a cop!" Brianca shouted out quickly.

"Put your hands up, now!"

"I have a gun. I'm detective Blair," she informed the officers.

Brianca slowly tried to remove her gun, and her eyes widened in horror as the cops pointed their weapons at her. In a feeble attempt to drop the weapon, she cried out again that she was a cop, as they unleased thirty-six bullets which entered her body, holding her body paresis until it fell in a heap. When she hit the floor, her riddled body twitched a couple of seconds then she was no more, *death by deception or friendly fire?*

Chapter Eleven

Sulaiman purchased real estate and homes in one of Raleigh's most exclusive neighborhoods. His reclusive life-style had been put on hold as he conducted business transactions. Several failed when a major opportunity arose in Japan. Every chance allowed, he swam the creek in the back of his 10 acre home, sharing it with ducks, swans, and other creature's nature. He had intentions on doing those things today, but a call from his wife shifted his plans, so he stayed at the house relaxing, eager to get things underway.

Sulaiman stood at the window with a water-pot, quenching his lovely Till and Sia's thirst. The plant grew facing the same direction as the sacred Ka'aba. He related to it, the main reason for buying it in the first place and both loved the morning sunlight.

He took to the front porch and with a drink of freshly squeeze lemonade, he lay on his hammock sipping slowly, sitting up when he noticed a money green Lexus creeping along the graveled drive-way. With anxious gleaming eyes, he stood full height, shirtless and chest swollen from the 500 push-ups and 500 dips he'd completed an hour ago. His chiseled square-jaw line, a chin a pro-boxer would love to have, nodded its recognition as the driver parked the car and got out, running to his outstretched arms.

He cupped her soft buttocks; his mind did anyway…..his eyes stayed glued to her every moment as she seductively took the steps to his arms. She wished she could have a glimpse of what his heart truly spoke, his conjugal rights were strictly for his wife, and the weeks had been brutal without her.

"Red, I've missed you."

"Sulaiman, I've missed you more."

He scooped her into his strong arms, spilling inside the spacious home just like he was going to spill himself into her. Clothes were ripped from each other's body in the heat of the moment. She kicked off the Cobalt flats, chucked the marble clutch to a nearby sofa, stripped off the beautiful white dress, no panties or bra, just the way he liked it. The zipper on his shorts was peeled, the fabric dropped to a heap as he stepped out, the only hindrance, his briefs. She dropped to her knees, slid them down, the large stiff erection stuck out long, and menacing to someone who'd encounter it for the first time. Her hot mouth burnt his beautiful flesh as she pushed the tip of her tongue inside the tiny hole to lap up the pre-cum that tasted so heavenly to her.

The love making was breathtaking, and every romantic episode left her begging for more. She loved spontaneity, and Sulaiman was all that and then some. After several hours of hot sex, both were sticky and sweaty. The husband and wife team dressed after another round in the shower.

The couple drove to downtown Raleigh to a posh luxury hotel for a quiet dinner in the back of a dimly lit lobby.

In the private section, they discussed the latest events. The look on his face showed he didn't approve of her actions.

Zohra went on to explain that Antonio had broken the family code out of greed, and although all money could be spent, all money wasn't worth spending, especially if it was made by snitching.

Zohra visited the turncoat and was placed in a room to be recorded, hoping their conversation would lead to valuable information of charges of conspiracy, to say the least, and possible murder charges.

Antonio sat there lying his ass off, while wearing the world's most hated Orange, even down to the ugly shoes. He duck walked in chains attached to his ankles and around the waist, then to the cuffs on his wrists. The cop stood closely as he eased himself onto the steel chair. The cop peered up; there seemed to be some sort of camera which snapped his attention, causing him to abruptly exit the room. He was wise enough to know he'd been told to leave so Antonio and Zohra could talk freely.

She said nothing as Antonio ranted non-stop, and she remained silent throughout the entire visit, showing no emotions nor did she respond to any questions or given advice. In fact, he became so upset and frustrated, he wigged out, causing her to end the visit. He knew he was a dead man. He became disgruntled by the things she revealed but understood what was done had to be in order to right all the wrongs.

The bishop may have gone to the extreme but she got the hacking idea from him. It placed fear in the heart of the toughest of men, but it sent a message and made a serious statement.

The crash through the house, she'd admit was a little too dramatic, but that was what she intended for it to be, shocking. The buzz on the streets was to let everyone know she'd do whatever necessary to get your ass, even if it cost her her life. Cats wasn't willing to commit suicide missions, this was a whole different level.

As to the Blair incident, she explained the digging she'd done which caused a heavy price for her and her boyfriend, at least she had spared the others.

So far, she was smug about the total outcome, even the Russians had sat down at the table with her. The two sides came to an agreement, and a joint network was put into effect, collaborating on hits to take out the remaining opposing fractions.

All wanted her to become the leader of the cartel once again, solidifying her rank with a table of seven and respectfully decline their offers. Citing her sole purpose for returning briefly, she gave a stern yet respectable admonishment of warning to those who sought to come after her, or her family.

The table gave their word no harm would come to her. She placed the only trusted person she could to the position, whom surprised her by asking permission to continue the War legacy of his 21 year-old cousin, the Captain's son Stephen 'Tug' War.

The group thought it to be ridiculous until they were given an impressive file, 15 kills and 1.5 million in sells since Antonio's unfortunate death of hanging in his cell.

This was a valuable asset to have, especially having a Captain as a father. The men decided to keep their networks as is, but welcomed 'Tug' to the cartels of the New York boroughs, leaving Zohra satisfied.

The meal ended and instead of returning back to the house, they got a room upstairs and made love again until the early morn. Zohra had a plane to catch and some unfinished business to attend to, the last of the clean-up. To ensure she'd get the job done and completed, Sulaiman sent some of his men back with her.

◆◆◆

Later that night, they drove to an area where six young men lined up on the streets, holding down their respective positions, making sells to any costumer brave enough to stop and purchase in the crime infested section of Queen's.

Zohra sat with gun cocked and a fully loaded clip, for days. She held up two fingers to the driver up front. The silent killer beside him in the passenger's seat with the AK-47 was ready to cause pandemonium and chaos.

The two watchmen posted on the rooftop of one of the buildings with their Kill Spencer tossed over their shoulders. They walked from end to end, talking in a heated debate over the greatest sneakers ever to be worn, neglecting their duties of looking out for cops and rival drug gangs.

Ready to sprint off at all times from the slightest movement of anything out of the ordinary were three youths with walkie-talkies, but the young punks were far too immature and inexperienced for what was about to happen to them.

It gave her the deepest joy to seek revenge for the death of her mother and those responsible for plotting to bring harm to her family. Besides, this would help the Russians claim more territory, should she need reinforcement for a full pledge scale war.

She hated that she had to lie to Sulaiman, but his reaction to her methods alarmed her, so she felt it necessary not to say anything else until every deed had been completed, which this was the last of her threats. Once this hit was placed in the books, she'd fly back to Raleigh to join her husband, and again she loved Raleigh, the little she saw of it, and couldn't wait to return.

Zohra entered the building, dressed like a social worker which was normal for this time of the month. The broken elevator indicated she had to foot it six flights up with wasn't bad considering she was in shape. She wanted to take the heels off but wouldn't dare risk being punctured by a heroin needle.

When she got to the top floor, two men guarded the entrance; one was getting his dick sucked while the other talked on the phone priming his dick for his turn. Neither saw it coming as she raised the gun and gave both men two shots a piece, head and chest wounds. The screaming female was quickly hushed with a vicious uppercut and a whack to the back of her head from the butt of the .45. She heard the footstep of the two lookouts running towards the door, ready for the iron door to swing open, and soon as she heard the door and saw the light of the sun, she unloaded the dead man's gun into the two caught off guard soldiers, neither had a chance.

Zohra dumped what was left of the corpse, snatched up the guns, money and cellphones, leaving the jewels and Kill Spencer's. She acted quickly, using the female's shirt to wipe the prints off, and then ejected the remaining bullets from the spent .9 mm. She used the unconscious female's hand to put them back in, working efficiently and diligently. This was done in order to ensure the awaken female wouldn't report what was seen, and if so, her reward for helping authority would be a trip downtown to explain how her fingerprints ended up on the bullets.

Once back downstairs, she dug inside her black bag and pushed two grenades inside her pockets. She walked bravely to the Benz parked on the street in front of a Brownstone that was used as a trap house. Four ballers were inside watching their money and discussing business moves.

Walking past, Zohra tripped and fell, and as planned the car door opened to assist her from the ground. She pushed him back inside with a bullet from the .45 and tossed one of the grenades inside of the vehicle. She got up quickly, and the same explosion was repeated by tossing another inside the door of the trap house, as she and Reason opened fire on the occupants running out to see what the commotion was.

The three young foot soldiers were rounded up and put inside a van then duct-taped with their heads covered up. The rest were in the first stages of rigor mortis.

Her teams piled in their respective vehicles and sped off to an undisclosed warehouse before the cops could come

The boys sat trembling as they awaited their fate. It was amazing how that youthful innocent quickly returned when you knew death was imminent. Snot and tears came from the 11-15 year-olds' noses as they answered questions by the tall, beautiful, white woman, while ten men stood with automatic assault weapons awaiting her command.

"As you see, I have the power to give you a second chance," she said, and then read off each name, age and home address. "Your cooperation spared your life and the lives of the ones you love. I give you my word. No one will find out the information you've given me nor will anyone know that you work for me now. The two hundred a week you now earn is a slap in the face. I'm giving you a stack each to go to school and get good grades. Straight-A report cards will get you five stacks, graduate; twenty, you come work for me, legit. Do we have an agreement?"

All three nodded vigorously, excepting their first payment from Nicolae.

"I want you all to notify me of anything you see or hear."

"Like a snitch?" one asked and frowned, hesitantly, knowing the consequences of being found out.

"No, a thorough spy, keeping tabs on the enemies," she corrected.

"Oh!" He understood, stuffing his money inside his jeans.

"If we don't hit the block, they'll question us," the fifteen year old leader stated.

Zohra continued to school, "As soon as someone questions you, after they leave, you call me," she said, nodding to Reason who gave each of the youngsters her number.

"I'll take care of them, as I've done the others. These men will not let anything happen to you. The block is hot now anyway. No one will dare try to sell drugs or put a team together."

"People saw us kidnapped." The youngest of the three finally spoke up. "What do we tell them?"

"Good thinking, little man. What's your name?"

"Vendell Taylor," he answered, stuffing his extra earnings in his pockets. He waved to Reason who'd given the youth an extra big face.

"Not your birth name, street name."

"Oh! Little Vee."

"That's better. Tell them when the van stopped at the light, you were able to slide your hands free and you untied the others, and at the next red light, you all got away and had to take the train back. Never deviate from the story."

"What's deviate?"

"Don't change the story or add to it. They'll know we lied if we do," the middle one said, receiving a nod as well for his smarts. He smiled as Reason fished into his pockets for a fourth time.

Zohra thanked the boys, schooled them thoroughly and told Reason and Nicolae to see them back home safely. The two men drilled the game to them until they let the trio out a block away at the arcade.

Chapter Twelve

When Zohra returned home, she was greeted by Kendrick who gave her some very disturbing news. Not wanting to discuss it over the phone with her husband, she called him to notify him that she was on her way out.

Sulaiman met the two at RDU. Kendrick had to leave and ready himself for college finals, ready to don his blue devil's gear.

Night fell fast and before long she was stepping inside of a luxury restaurant wearing gladiator boots, and holding onto a man who wore the same colors, causing eyes to stare and heads to turn. *Gosh, she missed that, relinquishing their privacy.*

Sulaiman ordered for the both of them, eating Casabas imported from Kasaba, Turkey. The meal was fabulous, and they capped the night off by meeting Reason at a popular night club in Raleigh, *Vegas* was packed to full capacity.

Sulaiman held onto his wife's hand as they moved through the dense crowd of jubilant party-goers.

The MC entertained the hyped audience, heads bopped to the cuts, mix and knock of the bass bumping from the speakers. The crowd was in frenzy, feeling the groove. Females popped their backsides and men clutched their hard wood, investigating all potential candidates for some late night action.

Unbeknownst to Sulaiman and Zohra, an enemy with a hair trigger temper and an impetuousness which kept her often clashing with folks as of late, lurked deep in the shadows.

Sulaiman noticed the glaring eyes several tables away and wondered what their reason for being there was. His askance eyes questioned, as Reason came over to join the couple with two females who were stunning. Evident pelf showed the high-maintenance females' love of the good life; they also understood they were not to be toyed with.

The females scanned Zohra from head to toe, and came to the conclusion that she was a carpet bagger from up north, stuck-up and conceited since she was on the arm of a fine rich Black man, but the two had underestimated her status. Although they'd been well informed, it was difficult to believe that a white female who sat inches away from them could be so deadly, while on the other hand, their eyes lingered on the brawny of a man whose brazen feats rang throughout North Carolina's streets.

Had not Temptation's mind been on Zohra, she would've been on the dance floor twerkin' it and doing several of the latest moves shown to her by Tracy Dimes before she'd left New York. Unfortunately, she didn't get the sought after information desired, but she understood Tracy Dimes' purpose for being there, and she took her job serious as Sulaiman gave his word to take her out of the ghetto and poverty state she'd been in, making her an organizer of events at his and his wife's restaurants.

The liquor and Molly she'd taken an hour ago had Temptation feeling some-type-of-way, and sitting just tables away to the right looking at his handsome self, only made matters worse. She couldn't take it any longer. She made up her mind to leave. Sitting there being constantly reminded of her lost definitely wasn't about to happen.

She noticed a group of thugs entering the building from where she sat facing the door. The men had to be known in the streets of Rough Raleigh. Fear and respect was generated, but there was one particular guy who stood out from amongst the rest, and the man oozed danger.

Temptation calculated him to be around 6'3" and maybe 195 pounds, give or take a little, definitely a hustler. He didn't appear to be a rapper or ball player, possible killer.

The two locked eyes, but his attention was snatched away by a light-skinned female, who he obviously didn't want planting her lips on his soft brown skin, leaving a smudge of lipstick as a trace of her haven been close to him. He quickly recovered by wiping the evidence away with a napkin handed to him from someone in his crew. He gathered himself, refocusing his thoughts back to the lovely beauty a short distance away.

*I can use him...*she thought, noticing the sneer she caught Sulaiman giving her.

She snickered at the sight. He paid her more attention than those at his table, and she planned to use this to her advantage.

The new prospect excused himself and moved through the crowd towards her. Knowing he was about to approach, his body language spoke volumes about the determination of his mission. The closer he got to her, it seemed the more handsome he'd become. His shoulder length dreadlocks made him look like a Lost Boys. With each step, the tight dangling locks bounced lively as his Nikes strutted across the floor.

He walked with Obama's confidence, with a swagger to match, definitely smooth-spoken. Straight and direct without any corny ass pick-up lines, he made his presences felt. "What's up?" He greeted, inches from her body, so close she could smell the mint on his breath. The stranger peered into her eyes; it made chills scatter over her body. Yes, he was very, very handsome, even more so than Sulaiman. "Who your lovely self with?"

"My lonesome, why?"

"Care for some company?"

"If it's just you, I don't do the crowd and I'm sure as hell not one of those chicks in here willing to fuck just to get high or noticed."

"Cool! What do you drink, Ms.?" He tossed the question out seeking a name as he extended his never-worked-a-day-in-his-life hand to her.

Holding out an even softer hand, she replied, "Temptation. My friends call me Temp."

"What does your man call you?"

"Well, if I had one, he'd probably call me a-freak-in-the-bed."

Laughter erupted from his chest. "Yo, that's some funny shit there," he responded. "I personally happen to love freaks, especially in bed." He gave her that look, "By the way I'm Left One."

"I take it that's not your birth name."

"Hell no, that's what the streets call me!"

"Well, what should *I* call you?" She retorted.

"Call me whatever you want while we're in bed, but around my boys, I'm Left One."

It was now her turn to laugh.

The drinks came to the table he'd claimed courtesy of his right-hand man.

"*Temptation*…..is that *your* real name?"

"Yes, to be perfectly honest, it is."

"I love it. *Temptation,*" He said the name as if it were a sudden revelation.

"You, do, huh?"

"I'm not going to waste your time. I'm digging you and I see us together doing some big things. And, if you'll allow me to, I'll prove to you that I'm the man you deserve in your life, now and forever. To be honest, I think your search is finally over." He spoke with an air of confidence.

"Who said I was searching?"

"The gleam in your eyes said it all when you saw a real figga. Look, lovely lady, I refuse to take no for an answer, for who knows if I'll ever get this chance again. No… I'm not letting you go."

"You're blunt and possessive."

"I happen to think those are great qualities."

Eyeing Sulaiman, she leaned over and whispered seductively in his ear. "I want you to show me how freaky you can get. And, if you can put all this ass to sleep, I might just stick around for more, much more."

Left One's eyes widened in shock, not at his game or how simple that had been, but at the fact she'd reversed it on him, now he had to prove himself.

"You smoke trees?"

"I burn the forest down."

"Cool." He nodded. "You ready to ditch this place? I know the perfect hotel."

"What about them?"

"Naw, they can't have any. You're all mines, but maybe if you're good, we can do a threesome later on."

Temptation cracked up. "You're so silly. Why one threesome? I thought you guys said *it ain't no fun if the homies can't get none.*"

"Hmmm, you do have a point there, but let's not get ahead of ourselves."

"Are you going to tell them we're leaving?"

"They know!"

Left One helped her with the light weight jacket. He reached for her hand the way men do when they're letting everyone know, *this here is mines.* He guided her through the crowd protectively, his men trailing close behind with several females in tow.

Temptation felt Sulaiman's menacing eyes on her back and began to throw and extra twist in her natural wiggle, shaking that ass the way a baby does a rattle.

Temptation shadowed Left One, sashaying out into the cool night weather. The April 6th temperature had been a far cry from the brutal New York City snow storms. Today's high in Raleigh had reached the mid-seventies, and the streets had been busy earlier with folks doing last minute shopping to get home and watch the hated Duke's get their butts kicked.

Left One tossed her the keys. He didn't even ask if she could drive a stick or if she had any license. The all-black Lexus sat like a Black Panther ready to spring into action. She wondered at his choice of make and model, always a story for one's ride.

She hit the alarm, opened the door for the both of them, and turned the radio; Jodeci' new, hot song bumped through the speakers. Finally getting around to it, Left One cut the T.V. on and watched the Carolina/Duke game he'd recorded about two weeks prior. Carolina started off with the steal and a fast break dunk bringing the Tar Heels to their knees. The game was fast paced to start with, but Duke took the lead in a furious attack. He sat in the seat as if it was his favorite spot, clicked off the T.V. and got into a deep conversation. Surprised she knew the game well, she promised to put him on with her uncle '347', and he knew he'd hit the jackpot. Everyone knew Tony Rains.

Left One loved the choice of hotel, luxury in a secluded area away from heavy traffic. Temptation parked the vehicle, paid the parking fees and as a cohesive unit after waiting for the last of his disciplined men and the respectively dolled-up women, they all filed into the hotel, the girls sashaying, others walking like the model types, beside what they hoped to be, their future baby-daddy's or a means to extra cash to ease the difficulties of life.

Once inside, Left One paid for his room instructing the men to behave. It was easy to get high and forget, 'No means No', and to wear protection. Although he was only a few years older, the guys looked up to him because of his realness and sincerity to those he allowed in his circle.

Temptation remained quiet but deep in thought, admiring the way he conducted himself. Left One separated from the others, knowing his goons plans were to indulge in a little group sex and illegal narcotics.

Surprisingly, the hallway was deserted as he swiped his key, pushing the door open to the twelfth-floor room. Temptation figured by him leaving the club so early, like most guys, he wanted to jump straight into bed. Temptation began to strip of her clothing. Left One kicked off his shoes, stripped down to his underwear and slid back onto the bed. He grabbed the remote from a nearby nightstand and turned on the T.V. and found the game, his team had the lead. This was just the way he liked it. His team winning, a beautiful woman in panties and some weed. What more could a man ask for?

Temptation dimmed the lights down low. Left One loved the image standing before him. Always two-steps ahead, he planned to do some very exciting things to the woman who stood before him. Temptation asked if he was comfortable, fluffing his pillow then stuffed it behind him as he sat up enjoying the beat down with a pleasant smirk at what Duke was doing to the team he despised.

"You want anything before I join you?"

"Naw, baby girl, I'm cool. You just bring your lovely self on over here."

He loved her voice, not too girlishly soft, and not husky on the masculine side. It flowed through his ears like a stream in the summer sun.

Temptation nodded, then slid in between the sheets, he follow suit. Her full, lush red painted lips touched his shoulders, causing him to forget all about the game. He wanted so desperately to crush his lips upon hers; the bulge in his brief could hardly be contained. The scent of her did things to him, screwing with his anatomy as her searching hand found his member and brought it to life with a few strokes in her soft gripping palms.

Left One's body reacted to her close proximity. It threw his heart into overdrive like tossing a match in a dry bush; his body became one big ball of flames. Her small white teeth bit into his muscled chest. She now straddled his lower body, guiding him into her warmness while peering into the depths of his liquefied eyes.

She flashed him a wicked smile as he entered the hot, tight flesh. The feeling was so good he closed his eyes and bit into his own lips, as she began to slowly rock back and forth, her voracious appetite for an explosive orgasm. The heat in her womb rose up, hissed like a serpent ready to strike. She grip his hands which were held over his head and began to slow grind in earnest, then a burst of flames roared, scorching and searing anything in its way. Trying his best to control himself, he lost it, and spun her over and took her from behind, just the way she loved it.

A couple of hours went by, both lay panting. Her CoCo Madimoiselle scented the room, mixing with the sex and sweat. Unlike an earthquake and tornado, the multiple orgasms came with warnings, and she laid there sensitive to the touch. He caressed her breasts, taking them greedily into his hungry mouth, biting, tugging and suckling the black hard berries. Temptation's moans were inhuman, his grunts animalistic.

Temptation snuggled up close, her mind on Sulaiman and why he acted in such uncharacteristic fashion. She didn't want to start another unhealthy relationship, but Left One was one of the finest men she'd ever been with. He was in top physical shape and he knew how to hit the G-spot like a punching bag.

The thug in him was a plus. He come straight in, placed his gun, a .9 mm to be exact, on the dresser, took off the platinum chains and chucked a wad of cash too. He must have trusted her, or had it been some sort of unclassed test she thought, either way, she wasn't going to go there, she had bigger plans and acted as if the pile didn't faze her, which really didn't, she'd bounce back with the help of her uncle, and she too… began to strip, placing her pearl handle .25 beside his semi-automatic, and an equally sized knot of cash, along with her jewels, then slid in the bed like, whatever. Then and there, he knew it was a match made in heaven. The two got it in again.

Chapter Thirteen

Zohra placed the dishes in the washer, and then turned to her husband who sat reading the Observer at the table. The breakfast she made was much needed, as she used every ounce of energy to keep up with her over-energetic husband. His expression, a far cry from the mask painted on his face last night while ravishing her body repeatedly.

"I saw her last night." The only sound there was, was the ruffling of the pages being turned and the noise of her tending to the kitchen. She spoke finally, breaking the silence.

"Saw who?" he questioned, having no clue as to what or who she was talking about.

"Sulaimon, don't play games with me. I saw you looking at her, Temp." It hit him. "I told you she was there. And yes, to be quite honest, I was very surprised to see her there."

"Were you jealous because of her being with another man?"

"Are you serious?" Sulaiman protested staunchly.

"Yes, I am. The way you came home and nearly pounded my guts out. I'd say, I think you were pretty damn upset about something."

Sulaiman chuckled, but Zohra found nothing funny. He placed the newspaper on the table, stood to full height and closed the distance between him and his wife.

He wrapped his strong arms around his wife's waist, drew her body to his and expressed himself from the heart. "Never think any woman walking God's green earth is superior to you in any way. I made a mistake that I'll regret for the rest of my life and believe me, the only way that snake was able to trick me into her deceitful web was to drug me, but I'll use that as no excuse, my flesh is part to blame. But as God is my witness, you'll never have to worry about me being jealous over another woman when my heart belongs solely to you." He smiled wickedly before continuing. "Plus, mind you, Carolina lost. And you know that pissed me off. Then I lost the deal in Greensboro. I guess… I took it out on you." He admitted. "On top of that, I have to travel to Kyoto."

Anticipating the trip, she hated the fact that he had to leave within a couple of days, seems like he'd been on the road more than in the bed, which got her to thinking, last night was one evening she'd never forget.

The drive home had been a hauntingly quiet one, and as he drove screw-faced, she let him vent, but she definitely planned to question the odd behavior as soon as possible. His blank expression was unreadable, almost zombie-like, but she trusted that whatever the reason for his uneasiness and often fidgeting, which brought about unwanted suspicious, he'd fight through it. He had to if he wanted to fight for their love, their family. But now with the truth out, he did take Carolina's lost serious.

Zohra knew she shouldn't have used such a poor choice of words, jealous wasn't exactly the word she'd searched for, although it came out the way it did. To be perfectly honest, she was the one who had been jealous, extremely, and she allowed insecurities to overcome her tested faith in her love. This love and relationship thing had been new to her, something she had to learn through experience. Her mother taught her a lot, but the romance department wasn't one of them.

With trembling hands that night, Zohra opened the door only to be ravished by a mad man of a husband who'd forgotten the words tender and gentle. Her clothing was ripped away forcefully. Forget about the expensive, slinky, nipped waist Reem Acra. Her lustrous hair and liquid eyeliner and deep-berry lipstick all ruined. He took total possession of her mind, body and soul. Hypnotized, yet fully aware as he stared deep into her beautiful luminous large doe-like eyes and held them captive while thrusting non-stop.

His need, she felt. The desire was raw passion beyond wild uninhibited sex. This was a level far greater then he'd ever taken her body to, the hot kisses to her mouth, neck and throat. She didn't put up any resistance, offering her body as if it was a ritual sacrifice. But her clothes hadn't been the only ones ripped and discarded.

Zohra tore at his shirt, revealing his bare muscled chest. She kissed and bit his nipples hard, shoving more wood into the fire. His fly came down, as he'd fumbled with the Levi button and shortly there afterwards, her grip circled the massive bulge as she freed it from bondage, yet incarcerating it into a hot mouth, but she'd been quickly denied of such self-pleasure as he so urgently needed her dewy flesh, wet and warm around his manhood.

His greedy mouth was buried in the soft mounds of her breasts. Wickedly his flicking tongue battled her taut nipples, causing her heart to pound like someone trying to break the door down because of a monster on their heels. The familiar warmness flowed through her veins, sending a signal to her sensitive core. Since there were no limits in the bedroom, nor any other location in the house for that matter, there was no telling where they'd end up screwing with his high freak nature. Anything and whatever he wanted to do, she was down for it, her body belonged to him to do as he pleased.

That night he'd confused her senses, suckling hard, then mixed things up with such sweet tenderness that she felt she'd died and went to paradise and back, it was maddening. Sulaiman catered to both breasts as if washing dominoes.

"Oh, God, Sulaiman, you're torturing me," she pleaded with moans.

"I mean to."

"I can't take this. It's too much." She needed him inside of her.

His eyes held her liquid blues.

His hard body pounded ruthlessly into her wetness, churning things inside of her. As she lay there taking the madness, it felt as if he was continually growing, longer and stronger. He was fortunate to be so blessed in the hung department; he ever tried to push his balls into her. Sulaiman wanted to be in her as much as humanly possible.

Her mind went over the positions they'd done last night. He was rougher than usual, but not in a disrespectable way, more like focused and determined.

Zohra was spun around, entered with an iron-rod, balls banging heavily against her flesh leaving the pale flesh bright red. She thought about her back, as sweat dripped from his sweat-laced forehead, the rug digging into her soft skin, rug *burns, she would be raw in the morning. She sucked on his stiff cock while parting her cunt inserting one finger at a time as his dick stretched her asshole. He couldn't get enough of its tightness and her gripping holes.*

Zohra didn't doubt her husband's words, but as long as Temptation remained in the picture, there would always be problems and she wasn't one for putting up with nagging gnats or flies both got squashed.

❧❦❦❦

Promise stared at her uncle in shock. Was he insane? She couldn't believe he'd requested this of her after only arriving in Charlotte an hour ago. Her two day drive from Texas had all but drained her. The last stop had been in Patrick S.C. to see an old friend, but other than that, she ate the highway up.

"Why can't you find someone else? It's not like you don't have a pack of wolves around here waiting for the opportunity to prove themselves," she blew, frustrated.

He was aware of her quitting the game and giving herself to Christ. Since Destiny had gotten herself killed at the club and had died in her arms, she'd given the life of the streets up. The bullets had been intended for her, and this she knew.

Reflecting on that horrible night, Promise had been stood up by Power for some type of paper-chase and she'd texted him over an hour and a half ago about her horniness.

Standing there deciding if she should leave or not, she let out an exasperating sigh and turned to leave, that's when she bumped into Master, a tall handsome D-boy from Fayetteville known in the street for his strict command of a hundred plus hustlers whose sole dedication was to him and getting money.

"Excuse me. Can I buy you another drink?" She acknowledged her clumsiness, taking a napkin from her pearl clutch and began to dab at the wet stain. "Come on in here real quick, I can take care of that," she said, not allowing him to protest, as she pulled him into the men's restroom which was surprisingly empty.

"You don't have to go through any trouble. It'll be dry soon. I might smell like a liquor house, but it's all good love. I'm not planning on staying that long anyway."

"No, I insist. You're too flyy to walk about wet and all... Take off your shirt." She pointed towards the old school-hand blow dryer.

He smirked. "What about my pants, they're wet too?" he asked, eyeing the stain where his bulge nestled.

In the dark club, he couldn't really get a good look at her lovely features, but now in the light, she was the hottest chick on two legs in the club.

Promise said nothing at first as if in deep thought, then walked over to the door, heels clicking the tiled floor with determined eagerness. Master thought she was leaving until she twisted the lock, securing their privacy. She walked back over to him, unbuttoned his silk $500 shirt, and let it slide off his shoulders. She tossed it to the floor then dropped her knees on it, and to his surprise, unsnapped the button on his black slacks, then unzipped the fly with her gripping teeth.

Promise loved oral sex and this tool dangling before her was just what she needed, and even longer than Power's, with a thicker girth. She licked it slow, and with eyes looking up at him, watched the excitement in his eyes come to life, as his manhood jumped like a recoil snake ready to attack.

He grew in her mouth, his boxers pulled down to his ankles, not even realizing when they'd gotten there or who had did it for that matter, all he could focus on was the thrusting rhythm he had, with his tightened ass cheeks and hands on his slender muscled hips. It didn't take long for him to coat the back of her throat, and as he grunted out the last of his climax, the pounding on the door came.

"Master, I know your cheatin' ass is in there with some bitch! You better come out right now or it's gonna be some trouble up in here!" the female threatened, flanked by two thuggish dames, bouncing from left to right, fists balled up, ready for a serious beat down.

The crowd formed at the door and Destiny peered around for her cousin so they could leave. She didn't want to stay if shit was about to pop-off, guns and black crowds didn't mix well with her. She asked around to a couple of familiar faces, trying to find out if anyone had seen Promise, and a tall-lanky dude smiled deviously.

"She trapped in the bathroom, 'bout to get them knuckles." He began to laugh. Destiny didn't see a damn thing funny. *What has Promise gotten herself into now?* she thought.

She began to thread herself through the crowd, trying to assess the situation, but was met with resistance when she approached the angry trio.

"Who the fuck is you all up in my business bitch!"

Destiny, known in the Queen's City for fighting shot back, "My peeps in there, and ain't nobody gonna lay a hand on her, not even you bitches!"

"What!? You got your people mixed up!" Trap Queen pulled a .380 from her waistline and without warning mean-mugged Destiny before turning the weapon she had pointed at her face. Then, she smirked as she dropped the aim to Destiny's gut and squeezed off two shots. Promise heard the gun shots but didn't have a clue as to who the shooter was or any of victim(s) if any.

Master ran to the door and unlocked it. His girl Trap Queen stood huffing, trying to get a good aim at Promise. All hell broke out, as security guards rushed to the scene. Trap Queen managed to disappear into the crowd with her girls, causing enough of a distraction to help her get away.

Her thoughts were interrupted by her uncle, bringing her back to the present.

"The guy who I had to make the run to got hit up with a gun on a humbug while stopping at a bullshit corner store to buy a pack of smokes. They had a checkpoint, and some asshole fled and it blew up the spot. Anyway, he made bond. The guy's solid, but with so much on the line, I need him to lay low until he takes care of his business. I don't want to chance it with a new jack or some trigger happy fool trying to make a name for himself." He breathed deeply. "I trust you and no one else knows about this drop."

"The guy who was supposed to drop knows, and that's more than enough." She knew shit was out of order, the charge may carry a nickel but a dime might get dropped, that shit don't add up.

"That's true, but one thing, he doesn't have any information on it. I called him earlier so he could come talk but as I've said, he never made it. Well?" He questioned, hoping the response was a go. "I know you can use the extra money. It's a cash deal for you, or four bricks, whichever you decide, but please don't keep me waiting, I need an answer, like yesterday."

He really hated to trust incompetent thugs. The stacks clouded her better judgment. If she was looking to gain that much off the delivery, she could only imagine how much of the coke she'd be sitting on. She took in a deep breath, not feeling this at all.

"Give me the information before I change my mind." She felt like Aliyah Blue in the novel *Why Do You Let Him?*

This was one of those times she felt she should have said no, but by her having plenty of experience in the business, there was no room for doubting or hesitating in the game. That familiar adrenaline rush kicked in and on instincts, she held out her hand and .357, dropped the keys to the U-Haul into her small palm, and ran it all down to her several times. With so large of a transaction, anything could go wrong and she hated to think about the what-ifs… a guaranteed life sentence. No less. But she had to go over all possibilities.

Promise understood her uncle's lack of trust in the business. But… with her being a reliable source, she had been his only option. There wasn't enough time to call Temptation, who had called about fifteen minutes prior from Raleigh to see if she'd made it home safely.

Hours away from the Queens City, she could call and tell her to meet her in Henderson, since Raleigh had only been 45 minutes away, but there wasn't any way to explain over the phone, and the way Temptation bragged about Left One's sexual feats, she discarded the idea, opting not to speak in code nor split the cash which was greatly needed. Only if she could us telepathic communication, she felt safer with Temptation than having being escorted by 10 armed goons.

She needed to do something to get Power off of her mind anyway, the cheating dog. So, with clarity and insight, she studied the routes and instruction until satisfied, asked a few questions, then she was ready to hit the road.

Uncle Tony handed her his signature weapon, a brand spanking new .357.

"What's this for? I won't need it."

"Just in case."

"What, you're Jaheim? You said, all I have to do is drive the location. There's a U-Haul already parked there with the keys in the ignition. Once there, make the call to a guy named Ro, who would be waiting at the 'Bullshit Pin' per my instructions. What's hard about that?"

"I'll feel better that's all," he said, strongly recommending it. Reluctantly, she grabbed it with a show of lack of enthusiasm.

Promise analyzed the entire operation on a broader scale; the cake alone was enough to net countless years but a weapon… it added to the list of charges like the knockout punch.

Thirty-minutes after Tony made the necessary calls, Promise took off. She had to leave. The more she listened to her uncle, the more she wanted to renege. With flaming eyes, she'd nodded to her uncle as he watched her wave good-bye. *Why did she have this gut feeling?*

Promise dug into the glove compartment, raiding it of its map. The GPS served its purpose, but she loved the old school way she'd been taught. She unfolded the large road atlas, scanning over it intently until she felt comfortable with her choices.

She took out her Smartphone, wanting to call Power, as her uncle had said, *"Just in case,"* he needed to know her whereabouts in case something went wrong.

"Stop thinking negatively, girl," she scolded herself, "no room for errors."

Chapter Fourteen
Henderson, N.C.

The decision not to call Power had been made, she thought it best not to until she'd returned back safely. He only had the slightest room to work with, one more mistake and their relationship would be history, and he'd never know of the good fortunes she'd acquired. The two needed a break from each other anyway, her friend Kiesha had told hear, and she'd agreed. He cheated on her first. Although they had both cheated on each other several times, hers had cost a life, and deep in her heart, she doubted her uncle had ever forgiven her for it. Trust and faithfulness had been thrown out the window long ago. Power found out about her first affair on the night Destiny had been murdered in cold-blood.

    Dangerously, taking her eyes from off the road briefly, she turned her phone off, cut the GPS on and began to search. The map of Henderson flashed on the screen. She zoomed in, weighing all alternative routes, turned towards the laptop on the passenger's seat, opened it and punched in the password then brought the club into view where Ro was supposed to be waiting. It wasn't that she didn't trust her uncle, and there wasn't enough time to check Ro's street credentials, besides the limited information provided to her of him putting in work in the streets and being a thorough D-boy. Representing the section of Flint Hill and Bankhead, if she'd checked around, she'd find out his name rang bells in the streets and prisons where he had left his mark.

Promise arrived in Henderson ahead of schedule. Needing a bite to eat, she pulled over to a restaurant 'Soul Delicious'. The food was absolutely amazing, making it one of her top five places. Finishing up, she exited the establishment with fifteen minutes to spare. She pushed it on the highway so she decided to gas up, stop at Party Pick, and to Westgate in the hood to see if anyone knew of the man called Ro. She decided to ask a female who'd just shopped at City Trend, around twenty-one, very beautiful, tall, light-skinned and had shoulder length, light brown hair.

"Excuse me, I'm from Charlotte and I'm looking for my cousin Ro. Have you ever heard of him?" Promise lied about the relation.

"Ro!" Her eyes lit up. "Everybody knows your cousin. He might be down on Lincoln Heights or Happy Hills." She gave several more locations and told some stories of shoot-outs and spots he hustled on, luckily she wasn't a narc, Ro's ass would be in deep shit.

Promise thanked the female and drove to the West end where she noticed a group of D-boys at a section called Spring Court, obviously on a paper chase. They all knew him. She stopped at a BP and sashayed over to some goons who said the same as the others, to a car wash where a T45, a SSR and Jag sat parked along with some flyy females entertaining the men. Promise went past her allotted fifteen minutes but who cared if he wanted it, he'd wait.

"Every hood is the same," she said, then stepped out of her BMW and walked over to the group bumping Jeezy.

She approached the driver in the Jag, "What's hood?" She greeted.

"You, sexy." He pushed from the Jag he sat on, eyed her from head to toe. "Nice ride."

"Thanks, but I'm not here to talk about my ride, but I do want to talk about Ro."

"That's my man. How you know Ro?" he questioned piquing his curiosity.

"I'm from Charlotte, I was supposed to meet him somewhere about fifteen minutes ago but….."

"Say no more!" he said then pulled out his phone.

She didn't want him to call Ro, but since she had that feeling about the way her uncle set the deal up, leaving keys in a U-Haul with bricks in it didn't sit well with her at all. The D-boy handed her the phone after the guy spoke briefly.

"Ro, speaking."

"I'm here."

"That's what's up," he said, keeping conversation to a limit.

She gave him the location to where she was and without further delay he ended the call and asked to speak back to his boy. She passed the phone back to the owner and waited patiently as they spoke momentarily. The talk ended and she got to meet the rest of the clique, all tight and hustled together. Promise liked the folks of

Henderson; the females were as thorough as the men and the guys about their business.

"There's Ro," the owner of the T45 said, pointing to a 760i.

"Wow! This guy don't play," she exclaimed, watching the vehicle the same color as the coke he was about to purchase.

Ro stepped out of the vehicle dressed as expensive as the ride he'd driven. His swagger matched his confidence, his razor sharp edge-up complimentary of Dice 'Em the hot barber on Eastside. His face had a mask of seriousness to it. "What's your name, sexy," he questioned, as he peered her in the eyes sharply.

"Promise, is there a problem?"

"Yeah, my man called me about 30 minutes ago..."

"Your man?" she questioned, thinking it had been her uncle.

"You spoke to his sister on the West end. Her brother noticed you were being followed because he tailed close behind."

"You're kidding right?" she asked, thinking it to be some game since she deviated from the course.

"Hell, no!" Woddie spat. "I don't think you're aware of it, but keep talking and acting natural, a blue unmarked car is parked across the street.

Frank white, one of the men next to his partner Kev spoke up, "Your Uncle is on some bullshit and he tossed you to the wolves. Are you aware that he was arrested last week with twenty Birds?"

"Arrested?! Hell no... You must be mistaken."

He noted the doubt in her eyes. Kev, who said nothing the entire time, handed her a news clipping. "He may be a small town, but news does travel. Now, we're not accusing you of no funny business, but we're good. We don't buy drugs," he said, in case she was wired, and she knew it by the way he said it. "We're just working guys, you be careful and make it home safe."

Promise had been in a daze, the betrayal of her uncle was difficult to swallow. She started to pick up the phone and blast him a new asshole and throw shade if she didn't get her money, but she didn't, she decided to wait until she got there before wigging out. Then it hit her, she had the money along with the guy he'd given her, it all added up.

That's why his punk ass gave me that gun! Oooh, I'm gonna kill him. she thought as she hopped into her BMW in shame, looking at the men who were about to purchase enough coke to flood Vance, Halifax, Person and Granville counties at $42,000 a brick, receiving 100 bricks on whole sell for $27.5 grand, luckily Ro and his men were on their game.

Promise planned to drive to the nearest store and trash the gun, preferably a restaurant so she could dump it off inside a waste can and take her chances with the case. Peering around for something to put the .357 in, she grabbed the brown paper bag she'd tossed into the backseat, stuffed the weapon into it and got out of the car.

As she locked eyes on the fast-food doors, cops poured in from every direction with semi-automatic weapons drawn in her face, feds threatening physical harm if she didn't place her hands behind her head where they could see them.

"Do you have any weapons on you or sharp objects?" a cop yelled, kicking her leg apart after forcing her to the ground, putting a knee in her back.

"No!" Promise cried out, infuriated. "You're hurting me. Is this necessary?"

"Shut up. I'm not going to tell you twice."

"Or what? I know my rights!" she thundered, hoping someone was filming it in case things get out of hand.

"There's a gun in the bag!" a female said, and then flashed her phone.

A tear rolled down Promise's cheek.

"I got the cash," another called from the backseat of her BMW.

The female smirked at Promise, that smirk one does when they let you know you done fucked up.

"Conspiracy carries life. You might have had a case if you wouldn't have taken that gun." She shook her head then frisked Promise before stuffing her into the car. It was over for her.

Chapter Fifteen

"I refuse to be weak… I refuse to be weak… I refuse to be weak!" Promise chanted like a mantra in the back of the squad car as it stopped at the final destination.

"Come on, Baby doll," a tall muscular agent said. He peered at the new Manola Blahnik heels she was wearing along with a baby doll mini that fit tight around her waist causing her bubble butt to stand out firmly. The crystal cloth had been taken by the female agent along with her other belongings.

He helped her out of the seat, loving her even-toned skin, its luminous glow and smooth face that appeared blessed to never have seen a day of acne. He got a peak of her cherry-red thong as she allowed him to assist her. However, she was unable to disguise her anger which showed she had screwed up big time. Even though she hadn't been charged or read any rights as of yet, patience in this case, was indeed a virtue. She prayed that God would help her through this ordeal. She hated she'd gone against the vow she'd made to Jesus. The hurt and fear of the unknown was a pain in the, you-know-what.

This didn't fit into her mapped-out scenario of earlier. Her conscious had given her a little heads up, but greed… that paper chase, had placed another human being behind bars.

For two, long excruciating hours, she sat on hard cold steel waiting for someone to come speak to her. The beating and banging on the door hadn't brought anyone running to check up on her, or threatening to shut her up.

Meanwhile, 'Tony, '357' Rains was down the hallway getting drilled for Promise not taking the bait as he'd promised she would. He was clueless as to way she had deviated from the path. She was his lifeline to freedom, and since his niece whom he'd adopted as a daughter had been killed at the hands of Promise, the bitter hatred grew like fungus on the floor of a brook.

"Be sensible Mr. Rains. Your niece is a young, beautiful woman who'll have no problems with incarceration. How old are you, 63?" the middle-age detective questioned. "What, she's 25 maybe a little older? She can do 10 years easily and still live a productive life. Now, we caught you red-handed. You've got statements that were written on you from several sources, plus this isn't the first time our informants have cooperated with us." He handed Tony a cigarette and kindly lit it for him.

Tony took a deep inhale of the Newport, allowing the smoke to fill his lungs, expanding, holding then slowly exhaling it to the left with twisted lips. He remained silent in his thoughts.

The lead detective in the case finally spoke up. "Now, you're a smart man. Hell, I've been trying to nail your ass for what?" He glanced at his partner. "Six years now?" His agent nodded. "But I'm afraid a charge like this will very well have you die in a stinking prison cell. Do you like the soaps? The guys there watch it religiously. Hard, cold-blooded killers reduced to the fuckin' day time soaps."

"Get the fuck out of here!" the agent said.

"I bullshit you not," he laughed. "What's that new show all the niggers like?"

"*Empire*," the agent said. He and his wife were also guilty of watching the show.

"Yeah, great show by the way. I've watched it a couple of times myself. You know, one needs all the information about your kind he can get. Black's finest, gays… drugs… betrayal and murder. Heck, one can see why it's a number one show."

Tony eyed the racist white agent in his eyes; he'd definitely have the last laugh in the end. Now, he was regretting his decision. They were going to eat Promise alive.

Business had been at its highest pinnacle for Tony, and with several of his trap houses booming, he couldn't afford to let everything he'd built go down the drain, it was too lucrative. The stick-up kids would have a field day once they knew he wasn't there to guard his houses. For years, the feds were unsuccessful in stopping the D-boy's he'd personally selected, but with all the recent arrests of three of his top gunmen within weeks of each other, he had to be careful. Word on the streets was a rival fraction was trying to take him down, the name *War* continued to arise.

After doing his homework, he found out the person behind it had been Sulaiman's wife's cousin, a ruthless killer only known by 'Tug' a killer *War*.

He tried to reach out to Sulaiman, who hadn't returned his calls about the matter, so he figured he'd had something to do with it once the number was disconnected, and no longer in service.

The set-up was one no one would ever expect, he did the unthinkable, yes and gave Sualiman and his niece up to the feds. Tony '357' Rains told authorities all about Sulaiman and the murders of the agents at the warehouse a year and a half ago, and the mall shooting which was a connection. He identified all suspects by way of pointing them out. He gave them a recording of the meeting between him and Sulaiman when he'd first came down from the Bronx searching for answers about Jamal. Tony knew to keep such valuable information just in case a day like this ever came about.

Tony used Temptation to get the whereabouts of Sulaimen, citing various reasons for the much needed information. Temptation told him of the mansion, the condo and had someone on the lookout for his home in Raleigh. The agents went straight to work with the leads.

He damn near had to beg Promise to make the run but she bit. He convinced her by telling her how he could trust her to run things while he pulled time. Giving up his niece should've been enough, he thought. At least to show them he meant business.

Temptation on the other hand was driven by greed. She'd be upset with him at first, but once he started rattling off figures, she'd definitely join the ranks as his most staunch worker. She had her problems but it never affected her abilities to make a dollar, fearless and strictly business, even though she hadn't been drug free long enough for his liking, especially to be trusted with major work. He knew time was limited, but he had to call her as soon as the interrogation was completed. If given the opportunity, once the eyes were off of him, he planned to sell everything, close shop and flee the country.

Danny Dollars was the first to be picked up. At 9:00 p.m., the black night held a quarter of a moon which sparked a dim light sharing space with limited stars, the perfect night for a sting operation on drug dealers.

Sergeant Isaac Diaz along with a joint collaboration of D.E.A. and the Gang Task Enforcement prepared their respective units to enter the apartment of Danny "Bills" Dollars' complex by way of tactically storming it and arresting anyone on the premises who didn't live there. Instructions were to lay everyone down once inside; it didn't matter if the occupants were elderly, women or kids. After the command to, *"Get down and put your hands where we can see them,"* was violated, the use of deadly force would be used without a second warning.

All units took their positions crouching behind their vehicles with assault weapons. The slightest movement, armed or not, would trigger the shoot-to-kill mentality, heightened amongst the men. International warrants were out for five men who were to be brought in dead or alive, many wanted the men dead.

The alley had been secured, his trap house surrounded, waiting for the "green light" the familiar signal to rid the world of one more criminal organization activity.

A dog barked erratically, trying desperately to get loose from its chains, snapping its teeth at the men. They stilled, hoping it would cease the dog and silence the noise, if not the red-nose pit that alerted the D-boys of their presence would be fatally wounded.

But Danny Dollars was always two steps ahead. Groomed in the streets of Queens, he lived for quick thinking moments. General-like, he stood while three women scooped several mounds of fish scales from a glass table into a plastic bag, tossing them amongst the others. The bags were for his runners who anxiously waited to make the quick dash as soon as they were handed off.

He peered at his watch; time was slipping away to the cops who were in position. There were wooden planks in the apartment to slide out of the windows for the runners who stood by with their bicycles to make a speedy getaway as soon as the units converged. They were ready to do what they were paid to do, get the dope to the next destination safely. The runners knew not to get caught, for their lives were on the line. 20 kilos of raw pink coke could get one's entire family killed. In Raleigh the coke was valued at 2 million dollars.

Finally, the women were finished. Danny Dollars watched the security cameras as they moved in closer. It was now or never. The women had their clothes on, each with a weapon so no one individual would have to take the entire gun charges by themselves.

Original pulled the rug back, revealing the square three-by-three wood board, an escape route with a drop down ladder to the empty apartment down below which was also a trap house where his workers rested up from their shift if they didn't want to drive home.

Danny Dollars aided the girls one-by-one down the ropes. Holding his Smartphone in hand which had a security program to the property, he watched the door to the apartment as officers attempt to kick it in.

Original already had the door bolted. The runners made their move and the girls made it safely down to the apartment. The battering-ram was completely ineffective against the four-inch thick steel door that had to be cut; otherwise it would need the use of explosives to gain entrance inside the trap.

The stoppage of the blitz was successful enough to allow them the much needed time. A flash grenade had been tossed through the window by Original who wore special made gloves and a gas mask stolen from Fort Bragg St., courtesy of an ex-soldier. These were no ordinary drug dealers, and the more one had his/her shit together in the game, the more prepared and the more money one would make, thus, the longer one lasted in the game. One had to out-last the others: stick-kids, snitches, crooked cops, informants etc.

Original, straight out of the Southside of Durham, raised on South St. where the streets bled red, had lived for this very moment. As long as his man got away, he was going to hold the fort down with bullets from his AK-47. A fierce gun battle pressured, as rumor had it. Original let off every single round besides the two he had left, right before being gunned down, and best believe he took several with him.

"Clear!"
"Clear here!"

"This one here is dead!" the agent said as he kicked Original with his boot, without checking to see if he had a pulse due to the numerous bullet wounds.

The house was thoroughly swept. There was evidence of someone cooking up dope from the warmth of the stove and glass coffee pots with hot water cooling down. Not a trace of cocaine, even the tables had been wiped clean.

Unfuckin' believable! Diaz thought while scratching his premature balding head. The K-9 were brought in, barking and pawing at the floor, revealing the getaway escape route.

The bastards knew we were coming, "Diaz thundered, peering at the security cameras. He glanced over to Original's twisted riddled body. The vest protected his chest area but the multiple head shots had left him unrecognizable. He sneered, then yelled at the two detectives a foot away, who were clearly in charge, "Detectives, these are not ordinary street thugs we're up against! I want their asses off the streets before the sun comes up! I'm afraid we might lose more men if we don't get them," he said, then shook his head at the dead agents, saddened that he had to notify his colleague's families.

Diaz had to give Danny Dollars kudos. Never in his years of working the force, had he seen such a well put together team, but he vowed to take him down, no one was bigger than the law, no one.

Chapter Sixteen

Danny Dollar drove cautiously, alert, yet inside, he was battered emotionally. He had to hold it together, for he was known for being incisive in all he did, but the girl, that was a different story. Her emotions were frangible like antique china plates tossed in the air by a drunken juggler.

He didn't want to appear too nervous by looking around for the cops, since that was a number one reason for blacks getting pulled over due to suspicion by overzealous, trigger-happy cops. Danny "Bills" Dollars drove the four-door at speed limit down Tarboro Rd, until he came to a stop for the red light.

Several patrol cars sped by, following three ambulances which meant there was a strong possibility Original was still alive or possibly dead, and he'd kept it hood by holding court in the streets, leaving carnage.

Danny Dollars glanced over to Original's sister, a lone tear slid down her smooth, beautiful, brown skin. She must have come to the same conclusion as he had…*her brother was no longer alive.*

Doing her best under the given circumstances to stay focused she continued riding, holding in her pain, until her thoughts were confirmed. She couldn't count the nights they all would sit around drinking, partying and bullshitting around, high off hydro. He'd make incendiary comments about going all out in a gun battle like the Boston bombers. Everyone thought he was just buzzing from the weed, but she had heard it often, even when he wasn't high. He didn't want to die of A.I.D.'s, cancer or an old man in a rest home; to him there was no honor in that, but to be talked about for years to come after his death, this gave his sick mind a greater high.

When Original volunteered to stay behind and hold off the cops, she begged him not to with her pleading eyes, but that look told her not to rob him of his destiny. He wanted to seal his own fate. The devious smirk and last smile let her know he was prepared for the long awaited moment. She had smiled back then climbed down the ropes. There wasn't a damn thing anyone could do for him right now anyway. Everyone knew exactly what they were signing up for.

Danny Dollars kept his eyes glued to the road, but his thoughts were on Tab.

The two had met in Goldsboro at a strip club while she was preforming seductively to Bump & Grind, an old school classic. He had been intrigued by the young, feisty stripper who worked the pole mesmerizing her fans by her acrobatic feats, which should have been on a video. Light skinned, slightly bow-legged with nice tits which were more than a handful. Her brown hair had been a little longer up close, shoulder length, with streaks of black highlights, so seductive. He had to go in deep, for when he left she was definitely leaving with him.

After her set, she vanished behind the curtains and the female a few feet in front of him serving drinks was called over and he whispered something in her ear, gave her a big faced hundred and she took off towards the back without pussy-footin' and brought back the requested female.

At first, she tried to act hussy-like, but he knew it was a front. He also knew he could break her, especially if she stayed and listened to his promises which she'd heard a million times before working at the club. Danny Dollars had her laughing, and her cheeks crimson from blushing at his filthy mouth, telling her the wicked things he wanted to do to her all night long.

For some odd reason, she believed Danny Dollars' words to hold her down. Tab didn't care too much about money. She had struggled all her life, so she learned not to live beyond her means. But she did want to try something a little different, something that would take her away from this place... she thought.

Tab, giving into yet another D-boy with dreams of being on kingpin status, fell for his words, ready to lose the loser she had at home sitting on his natural black ass while she made the cash.

The Durhamite needed stableness in her life. Her good looks would ONLY go so far, and the untapped potential she had, was put on hold because her boyfriend wouldn't get off his lazy ass to work so she could go to Wayne Technical College. The lame so-called boyfriend was faker than the $50 nails she wore.

She made up her mind, gathered her things and left the owner barking obscenities at her back. Tab didn't even go home to get her belongings that night; it didn't even obnubilate her mind on the decision. Straight to the hotel is where they went, and only because of the time did he not make the drive to the state's capitol.

Danny Dollars sexed her until check-out time the next morning, and after they were both pleased, he took her to get her clothes and valuables from the house. He reluctantly drove her over where she was lambasted by Daryl, who, in turn, was beat within an inch of his life for getting all up in Danny Dollar's face.

Tab knew Danny Dollars was about his business and the fact that he was driving a hundred-plus grand vehicle spoke volumes, especially through the murderous hoods of Durham where one would get carjacked over far less. Her hood, one couldn't get caught slipping pushing wheels like his, but he was known throughout the major cities for squeezing the hammer.

Overnight, Danny Dollars became her addiction, not some quick fix, using his silky smooth lines, his charm and hypnotic savviness. He kept his word, moving her to a new environment, in the high-class section of Rough Raleigh, introducing her to his suicidal life-style, and a life many young black youth were dying to become a part of, dreams of spending stacks of wealth on bitches and cars as they say, clothes and clutches, jeans and dresses, jewels and diamond rings which costs over six-figures.

She tried to avoid the life for years. Her in-and-out of jail brother had helped her make her mind up a very long time ago, seeing him take charges for goons who'd shitted on him. They'd leave his broke ass in the Durham County Detention Center unable to make a $5000.00 bond. Lord knows if it ever reached a quarter of a million on up. Loyalty towards the wrong people kept him on the wrong side of the law, and she'd told him about her new boyfriend and gave Original the number. Knowing Original's plight, he invited him over for dinner and told him to bring a female of his choice. Danny Dollars understood the struggle, the streets, and planned to get it while it was for the taking. None of them were born with silver spoons but all planned to die with platinum chains.

Once at the posh condo, Danny Dollars gave Original the opportunity of a lifetime, and within six-months he went from selling twenties to grossing $20 grand a month as Danny Dollars' right hand man, his trigger man, thus eating good in the hood now.

Tab sat thinking about how Original had brought their cousin over because he couldn't find a female who'd come unless they were guaranteed a slice of the pie, boy did they lose out.

Patricia was welcomed by Danny Dollars. He loved her dark complexion and smooth like milk chocolate. She was thick, with curvy hips and an ass that bounced like a ball player trying to dribble two basketballs at the same time. Your eyes would get crossed over as if John Wall had put a move on you, if you stared too long. Danny Dollars moved her in just to see her walk around the house. At first Tab didn't mind, they were blood and both had been through a lot together, but from experience she thought it best to get Patricia a D-boy to keep her occupied, especially since the occasionally threesome ended up with them sleeping together on the regular. Danny Dollars started calling her Black Bubbles; her real ass was so perfect, the symmetry seemed fake making one want to touch it to see if it would burst.

Danny Dollars had Tony Killz over one night, he'd came from Charlotte to talk about networking with each other, that way the two could set up trap houses along some of North Carolina's busiest cities like Charlotte, Greensboro, High Point, Winston-Salem, Monroe, Fayetteville, Rocky Mt., Greenville and Asheville.

Tony Killz and Danny Dollars planned and plotted for four hours until they were convinced it would work if they involved the other excluding Sulaiman. They all knew he wasn't going back to the streets after making legit capital.

Tony Killz had some kin folks in some of the smaller areas, areas that couldn't be slept on like Wilson, Wadesboro, Rockingham, Burlington, and Reidsville where your onion would get peeled being on the wrong side of the tracks.

Tony Killz couldn't believe his eyes when the two women walked in dressed as if they'd been with Uncle Luke. He hopped up quickly, "You gotta be kidding me, cuz. Who's this sexy devil?" he said, poking fun at the 'we're no angel's movement'.

These women were absolutely voluptuous and could have easily been on one of the commercials.

"Tab, the one on the right is my girl." Patricia said nothing as to the comment. "The female beside her, is her cousin, Black Bubbles."

"Why they call you black Bubbles sexy?" Tony Killz inquired.

"Show'em why," Danny Dollars said, walking over to her, spinning her around for all to see.

"Damn!" was all he could say as he squeezed his cock.

Black Bubbles smiled, she loved it when men gasped the first sight of her ass.

"Do you like what you see?" Danny Dollars asked, smiling himself because he'd been all up in it.

"Does a dog in heat hump ass?" he spat wisely.

That night Tony Killz knew she'd be his forever. Regardless of his situation back home, he wasn't about to let that ass be seen by no other man but him, whatever the cost.

Black Bubbles had her mind on Tony Killz. She pulled out her iPhone and called her lover to warn him, just in case there was some sort of connection.

Tony Killz stood looking down below at the cops entering the building, wondering who they were after. He kept no guns or drugs in his home and conducted no illegal business there, and he always made sure Black Bubble abided by his strict rules.

Tony Killz answered the phone, "Tony…"

"What's going on?" The cops are swarming the building. They got Danny Dollars' houses on T.V. being raided. We don't keep shit here and nobody better not know about this place either," he said, shy of accusing her.

"I never brought anyone up there and there's nothing inside the condo but my clothes."

Black Bubbles heard the door being kicked in and agents yelling for Tony Killz to drop his weapon. A quiet passed, the sound of gunfire, then a silence before the agents said, "Man down!"

Black Bubbles knew from the rounds fired, Tony Killz was a dead, she also knew he'd never kept weapons at the condo.

"Whoever this is, we're coming for you," an agent said, and then the line went dead.

Black Bubbles clicked off and told Danny Dollars what had just transpired. Danny Dollars pulled over to the next exit, she needed to be rid of the device. They had kept mason jars filled with acid inside a vehicle at the parking lot of a Wendy's. She'd drop the iPhone inside it and dispose of it to the nearest trash bin. Black Bubbles remained silent as she climbed back inside the waiting vehicle with nothing but murder on her mind.

  If only she knew Tony Killz' wife had been stormed by Federal Agents just hours ago on her way to Charlotte. His wife was furious that her children had to go through the private searches, enduring the gun toting agents shouting disrespectful threats and the ram shacking. Finally, she'd had enough and disclosed to the authorities her husband's whereabouts and the location. She had private investigators follow his cheating, adulterous ass. The city council woman had just filed for a divorce earlier that morning and with perfect timing, he would get those papers served on him in the county jail.

  Karen hated that their once fairytale marriage had come to a nightmarish end. She helped him through his criminal activities as much as possible without breaking the law, urging him to straighten up and fly right. It became obvious that he had no immediate intentions of leaving the streets. With a 1.9 million dollar home in an upscale neighborhood, several barbershops, a mom and pops store as a front, his whorehouse condo which was in her name and the three luxury cars all financed and paid for by her multimillionaire banker father, she stood to gain a significant amount of wealth from the funds he'd placed in her bank account, making a way for her to provide for their children's future.

Chapter Seventeen

Danny Dollars was petrified. What the hell was happening? First him, now Tony Killz, he had to check on his cousin. But first, he needed to see if his coke had made it to its destination safely. He dialed the number to his secret trap house and his girl, Baby Blue, answered the phone.

"I returned 20 large pizzas back because they were cold. I'm just checking to see if they've arrived yet."

"Yes, Sir, all twenty are here. Sorry for the inconvenience, is there anything else we can do for you?"

"That'll be all for now. Thank you."

"Thank you for doing business with John's pizza." Baby Blue disconnected.

"Is everything alright?"" Tab asked, seeing the worried expression on his face, somewhat.

"Yep, now I gotta call Sage, see what's good with him."

The call was made. Danny Dollars waited, one more ring and he was about to hang up.

"Yo, son, this better be important!" Sage said, as he yelled over the pounding bass that knocked relentlessly through the speakers.

"My figga, they just ran up in my shit, and minutes later… cops killed Tony Killz' ass at his condo!" He barked into the phone, "Is that important enough for your fuckin' ass?"

"Sorry about Tony Killz, cuz. But you know I been out of the game for a year now. What's all this gotta do with me?" he questioned, not meaning to sound so insensitive, but wanted his cousin to know freedom or life. He had tried many of nights to convince Danny Dollars to give up the street life, but he chose to keep it gutter. Compared to what they were making, Danny Dollars and Tony were making crumbs, but it wasn't about the money, not with them. It was the thrill that came along with the lifestyle. He'd known his cousin would come face to face with this day. He planned to distant himself as far as possible, call it what you want, legit money was far better than being in prison for life, degraded to hustling for smacks and cigarettes. And he sure as hell wasn't about to be added to the statistic of another brother dying on the block chasing paper.

The lovely brown-skinned female between his legs giving him monster head, had solidified his decision a year ago to leave the streets alone. Listening to Danny Dollars babble on had him thinking about the business deal Sulaiman had called him with earlier that day. He'd agreed to join in and flip a cool million from three back. The game never changed. After hanging up, he paid the conversation no mind, his focus was on the 38 triple Ds before him, a very beautiful female from Los Angeles. Her zodiac sign, Sagittarius, and in the bed she represented the horse to the fullest, stamina and very energetic. The 4'll baby doll without heels boast of measurements 38-33-44, her nationality, Puerto Rican/black.

The king-sized bed made him feel king-like as he lay back comfortably, raking his fingers through her long, jet black, oily Puerto Rican hair. He knew he had to leave a card for her while in Japan for her to get it back the way it was, but it was money well spent.

Sage's mouth watered as he eyed her soft puppies. He wanted so badly to get in between those bouncy large breasts and hump at least two nuts out. She was such a turn-on. *The hottest chick on two legs,* he thought. Racks' baby bottle nipples were his paradise on earth, and to hold them we're heaven. He loved the way her nipples protruded through her bras or blouse; they stood out like headlights and he was the deer caught in them. The taste of them, her hot flesh, the scent of her breasts, especially when they were sweaty and sticky from his thick white goo lathered into her skin like fine expensive lotion. The way they looked swollen, the weight and hardness of the nipples at peak. It all turned him into a mad man.

Racks climbed onto the bed, straddled his lap and squeezed both of her breasts. With lust laced eyes, she waited on him to suckle them the way she loved them to be pulled and tugged on. She laid her body onto his, loving the way their combined flesh felt, his hard body beneath her softness, soon she'd be wrapped around him like a soft blanket.

Sage pushed her body up slowly, then spat on her warm hard nipples, the same way she did his cock head. He watched her tweak them. His favorite part came up. He began teasing with trailing kisses around the orbs, his tongue dragging lazily on the swelled bumps, causing moans to escape those painted cheery lips. He leaked from the tip of his cock, ready to hear her cries of pleasure. He'd memorized every single sensitive spot of her creamy soft skin. Her body shuddered at the anticipation of his dick sliding in between her legs. Again, he licked her nipples then served the other parts of her body, driving each other wild with that familiar desire for one another. His need to be settled deep within her body and moving as one was great. The feel of her small soft hands roamed all over his muscled black skin, thanks to Sulaiman's insane work-outs. The lust for him was brutal, demanding.

He allowed her heat to consume his cock as he straddle her chest, punched her breasts around his think long member and began to slide back and forth, as if his thickness was inside her tight warm pussy. He closed his eyes, imagining wet-tight-gripping cunt and within 60 strokes, he gasp and that caused him to lose it. *One down, one to go,* he thought.

He held her gaze, their bond a degree over love, more powerful than lust or passion. Each touch, or rather thrust, raised the baby hairs on her body. He let her take over, squeezing her jugs together and tugging on her taut nipples, bringing an erection back, as he slid in the loose goo, a natural lube. The heat liquefied his cock, her eyes closed, body tensed, he knew she'd come.

On cue, Sage began to increase speed. She always wanted that after she'd cum. Switching gears, he sweat hard, she too as he whispered freaky shit in her ears. Her tongue lapped at his pee-hole, and having had enough he crawled down her body, slid into her hotness, trying to reach her feminine core. His hips bucked back, trying to contain the assault, losing the battle.

"Shit, oh shit! You fucker, hold it right there! Fuck!" she said, grinding hard.

Sage cupped her ass, she gasped at the sensation that travelled throughout her body. He was devouring her soul like a black hole. He banged her out, head knocking on the headboard like the bass thumping in the background.

The phone rang again, but there was no way he'd stop now, not while he was about to answer his need.

"Baby, answer it. I need to use the bathroom, anyway."

Dick harder than a West Coast gangsta, he reluctantly pulled out, staring at the beautiful 38s. "Hurry, up. Don't make me wait too long."

Racks squeezed a handful of hard man-meat, "I wouldn't dare."

Sage slid into his slippers, watched Racks spill from the bed, walking bow-legged. She thought she had all the sense, he knew where she was headed, to freshen up again and take a Molly to keep up. She had bought some toys for him about a month ago, and loved the way he'd used them on her, she grabbed them also. He peered at the screen; it was his next door neighbor. The dude was about 17 years old. Sage had paid him to keep the car, yard and pool clean, but why was he calling at 10:45 p.m.?

"What's good, B?" Sage questioned, hoping he sounded annoyed.

"The F.B.I. I got your house surround. I believe their getting ready to kick in the door."

Forgetting about the two 38s in the bedroom, literally, and no longer referring to Racks' breasts, but the two weapons, one his and the other hers. He knew they didn't have anything on him. So, he went back to the room and grabbed his shirt and jeans in haste, not wanting to have to fix a booted-in front door.

Racks came out of the bedroom. "Put some clothes on, we have visitors."

He peered at the sadness which quickly turned to anger in her face. She'd put on lipstick, perfume and editable thongs.

"Damn!" he said then stomped off wondering what kind of mess his cousin had gotten him into.

Just as Sage twisted the doorknob to let them in, they wrestled him down to the floor, thinking the cell phone was a weapon. Luckily, he wasn't shot unarmed. Taken down, he struggled to get lose, but found it difficult with knees in his back and shoulders, pending him to the floor.

Racks heard the commotion up front, ran over to the pillows and took both guns from beneath them. She then checked the safety; she loved the thrill of fucking with a loaded gun next to her head, it heightened her orgasms.

She headed for the living room after tossing a shirt over the weapons, and just in time. She found herself with semi-automatic weapons drawn on her.

"Freeze!" the agent screamed.

Racks threw her hands up and submitted to the man-handling of the agents who roughed her down to the carpet, rug burning her cheek, with a knee in her back. Barely able to speak, she cocked her head to the side, and with a half-whisper, she mouthed, "I got your gun."

He closed his eyes. Her gullible ways had gotten her a gun charge, but what angered him the most was the salty glares, and the way they struggled with her. She kept saying, *my stomach, my stomach,* but her pleas went unheard.

"Stop resisting!" a tall white agent barked.

"Get the fuck off her, she will!" Sage fired back.

"Shut up asshole, or I'll put a boot in that trap!"

Racks tried to reach for the guns which pressed into her, cutting her flesh.

"She's reaching for a gun!" the trigger-happy agent warned before letting off a round, causing the rest to react and riddle Racks' body, killing her.

Sage tried to shield her from the fire and took six shots. The room smelled of gunpowder; a pool of blood outlined the two twisted figures.

The atmosphere turned morose and the body cameras didn't do a damn thing to stop the killing.

Billy had been instructed to call Danny Dollars in case anything should happen to him, the moment had now arrived. With Fidgety hands, Billy dialed the number he'd learned to memorize.

Danny Dollars peered at the number and murmured to himself, "This isn't good." Quietly, he listened attentively, and after hanging his head down low, casted a furtive glance at Tab, closed the phone shut forcefully then threw it to the floor with a rage in his eyes unlike one she'd ever witnessed before, "Racks is dead, Sage is on the way to the hospital, I think Rex…" he said and paused somberly before straightening the rearview mirror to give Racheal's sister Charmaine who sat in the backseat the entire time trembling, the news.

Charmine, thought about the traumatic change in her sister's life. Just last night, she'd talked about marrying Sage. She had just graduated from nursing school and they planned to throw her a surprise party where Sage was going to secretly propose. Racheal had lived a mundane routine long enough, and Sage put her through school and took her off the streets, leading by example. She also was a baby in Christ, her only sin and weakness was Sage. Now, it was too late to travel that narrow path to eternal life, affliction strewn in her pathway. *How could someone who gave so much of themselves to others be killed so violently by those who were supposed to protect her?* Everyone knew the way out of the game was death, but what about those who weren't in it? Life to Danny Dollars seemed unfair.

Charmaine's eyes widened. The recognition and warning had come a nan-second too late. "Watch out!" Charmaine yelled instinctively, bracing for the direct impact of the collision.

Danny Dollars worked the six-speed stick down, shifting, as he stomped on the breaks yanking the steering wheel to the right with the failed intentions of avoiding a head-on crash. But the decision to do so caused Tab to take the blunt of the force.

The female driver who'd dropped her cell phone quickly bent down to retrieve it from the floor liner, veered into the path of on-coming cars, ramming the front-end into the right passenger's side of Danny Dollars vehicle, folding it, twisting the metal into a V-shape.

Danny Dollars' air bag kept him from being ejected, but Charmaine hadn't been as fortunate, failure to wear a seat belt caused a fatality.

A guy who happened to be an off duty cop witnessed the entire accident. He also observed a black male, five-foot-nine, and 185 pound wearing all black, white sneakers and carrying what appeared to be a back pack fleeing from the scene.

The broken arm, cuts, scrapes and bruises to the facial area hadn't mattered to Danny Dollars, he just couldn't get apprehended with the guns and quarter of a million in cash. Danny Dollars and Black Bubbles made it out of the wreck. The white guy hadn't seen her crawl out from the back seat.

With only a block and a half to go before reaching his house he was approached by a neighborhood kid on a bike, who would make runs for him to the corner store for cigarettes and snacks. He was forewarned that his home was being raided by the cops, and they were asking folks of his whereabouts.

No one knew of this place, and it left Danny Dollars puzzled as to how the authorities had found it out. He peeled off two big faces and gave them to the youngster and told him to watch the house for him until they left. He gave Cory a pat on the head and told him there was more where that money came from if he kept his trap shut. Cory rode back in haste, he hated cops anyway.

The two dipped inside of a clothing store, quickly finding something to change into. After purchasing a set of clothes, he dialed a cab and watched out of the window as the ambulances sped past, praying Tab's unbreakable spirit would keep her alive.

"From here on out, it's me and you against the world. So, seize the opportunities thrown at you, and if you continue to prove loyal, you'll be generously awarded," he said to Black Bubbles.

He needed them to work together like a well-oiled machine, in a cohesive manner. From past experiences, she knew there were no limits as to how low someone would stoop when on the run, and she wasn't about to face the RICO law because of him being a most wanted criminal. As soon as she got the opportunity to get her hands on the cash, she would cash in on the reward. And without saying, it would be him or her. She knew without a doubt, defeat wasn't agreeable nor was prison.

Rocking on his heels with hands jammed in his pockets, his main thoughts were on Tab, and he had to get to the hospital to make sure she was alright. The cops didn't know about her, at least that's what he suspected. To make sure she wasn't guarded by cops, he told Black Bubbles to take some money and find them a hotel room somewhere. He also told her if he didn't call her within an hour to call him and make sure he hadn't gotten locked up. Reluctantly, he gave her the money and told her as soon as he got to the hospital, he'd get in touch.

The cab pulled up in front of the store and he sent her on her way.

Danny Dollars prayed she'd didn't take the money and run. She couldn't be that stupid, knowing he knew the places she hung at. He watched until the cab vanished around the corner then made his move to his neighborhood.

Sporting a Vince Camuto black leather jacket, dark Ray Ban sunglasses, near-white stonewashed jeans and a white wife beater, he murmured, "Man, I might've fucked up."

Once to the corner store, he saw Cory squatting down rolling dice with a group of four, his Cadillac bicycle on the kick stand.

One teenager was heard questioning Cory, "Ain't that ya' man?"

"Yeah," he replied, "I'll be back." Cory scooped up his winnings.

What's hood, Bills?"

"I'm good, those pigs still squealing around my house?"

"Naw, they been gone, but they got a car parked across the street in case you show up." Cory peer him in the eyes, "They had dogs and shit all up in there, came out with a few bags and a computer."

Danny Dollars knew he was clean. He kept nothing at his main house. For all he cared they could search all they wanted, he just needed to know what they were searching for.

"You got your bike?"

"Yeah, it's over there, why?"

"Give me a ride pass my house. I want to see shit for myself."

"Man, nigga's gonna think we gay and shit."

"Fuck what them broke-ass fools think. Anyone of those nigga's gonna give you a stack for an hour's worth of work?" Danny Dollars said, now peering into Cory's crystalline blue eyes.

Cory tried his best to act black, the only white boy in his clique. He thought long and hard about the decision he was about to make. He knew Danny Dollars was a thug to say the least. His father had warned him about being around *the black guy next door*. Besides, his father still didn't believe Danny Dollars was his real name. He knew his mom liked Danny Dollars, often catching her squinting through the blinds at him. From her room, she had a direct view of his master room, where she witnessed some of the most mind blowing sex ever. She wished Frank would screw her in such fashions, or in the ass like Danny Dollar did his women.

To save face, Cory peered back to his boys, "I gotta handle some business. Here's some change, get us some Indo. I'll be right back."

When the big-faced hundred he'd tossed hit the ground, it was quickly scooped up, and down to the weed spot, four blocks away, they ran. Cory had earned his spot amongst the crew. With frequent ass kicking and a few breakings and entering, he became *that cool ass white boy*.

Just like Cory said, a car was parked across from the house, inside, two plain clothes eating and drinking.

Some stakeout, he thought as he rode pass on the back seat with Cory's fitted cap pulled tightly down just past his eyebrows.

Cory's mom saw the two, shaking her head, as she stood on the front porch. She went inside the house and grabbed her cell phone and keys.

Cory knew he was busted, big-time. His mother's dagger stare spoke volumes, but to his surprise, she said nothing. He prayed she didn't snitch, had it been his father, the matter would have been settled, as he bolted across the street to inform the authorities.

He saw the tension lines zig-zag deep in her forehead, but he kept peddling as Danny Dollars gave instruction to get them off the block and to the nearest store so he could call and find out what hospital Tab had been taken to. He explained in detail, that he needed Cory to go into the hospital and see if the place was surrounded by cops, and if Tab was still alive.

A silver Benz pulled up beside him and his heart almost stopped. His mother was motioning for him to pull over. Cory debated on whether to stop or not, a grand of cash was on the line. He was 16, two weeks shy of turning seventeen years old; worse-case-scenario, the car he'd been promised could be taken away before receiving it for graduation, or he could possibly get sent off to some private school out in Rhode Island with his military uncle, Dan.

"Pull over."

"What?"

"Go ahead. Pull over," Danny Dollars said, holding on as Cory slowed his peddle. "See what she has to say. It can't be too bad, the cops aren't following her."

"You sure?"

"Yeah," Danny Dollars said, staring Wendy in the same colored eyes as her son. "Over there!" He pointed to a storage room parking lot.

Cory made his way to the abandoned parking lot, his mother pulled in directly behind him. Danny Dollars was the first to dismount.

Wendy stepped out of the vehicle and walked straight up to Danny Dollars and said, "You know I can have you arrested for having a minor help you elude arrest."

"Mrs. Morris, you're absolutely correct. I won't contest to what you've said but if you allow me a couple of seconds to explain my inexcusable actions, and still don't agree, I'll help put the bike in the back of the trunk, get in that back seat and let you turn me in to the proper authority."

Wendy watched her son's mouth widen in shock. She too, had to admit shock, and by his conversing, he didn't speak the urban trash her son had been so obsessed with.

"You have two minutes and this better be good."

"Thank you, Ma'am. Sadly, I can't trust anyone besides your son. I'm sure you've heard the terminology *Keep it real.*"

She nodded, arms folded over her generous breasts.

"Well, I was conducting business," he said, not disclosing what type. "And just as I was about to prepare for my business trip in Japan tomorrow, the cops kick in my girlfriend's home, waving guns like crazy." He lied about that part. "My friend is a dealer. Yes, I know it, but I grew up with this guy and even though I don't sell drugs, I wouldn't abandon a friendship. True friends are rare, regardless of their luggage. Anyway, my friend and his girlfriend were murdered by the cops, unarmed…," he said, and then sighed. "I'm not using race, but as of late, a lot of white cops have been killing us blacks, so we managed to escape barely with our lives, that is, until I got into a wreck. They rushed her to the hospital."

"Mom, that's where I was taking him, we can't trust anyone."

"Especially trigger happy cops." Danny Dollars shook his head in disgust.

Wendy saw the sincerity in Danny Dollars eyes, and her son really wanted to help his friend. "Put the bike in the trunk."

"But mom," Cory protested.

"I'll drive you to the hospital. My best friend is an agent with the FBI. Once we're through checking up on your friend, I'll make a few calls and we'll get to the bottom of things."

"What if they lock me up?"

"For what? You said you didn't do anything. And if you have, I'm quite sure you're not stupid enough to get caught on camera or selling to an informant."

She was right. They didn't have him on camera, and hand to hand sells were out of the question.

"Alright, Mrs. Wendy, I trust you. Let's go." He smiled, noticing the erect nipples he'd focused on and she jutted out her chest, hoping one day more than his eyes would be on them.

Wendy climbed back into the driver's seat, knowing her husband would be furious at her actions. It was probably the reason why she did it, fed up with the long lonely night and no sex for weeks.

Danny Dollars had forgot all about the time. He was supposed to call Black Bubbles ten-minutes ago.

With ease, Danny Dollar placed the bike inside the truck.

"Dude, you were totally flirting with my mom right in front of me."

"No disrespect, Cory. I think your Mom's cool," he said using the word cool instead of hot.

"I can tell she likes you, too. Let's find out where your girls at, so we can find out if she's alright."

Danny Dollars slid in next to Wendy. As she drove, she found it very difficult to focus on the road for staring at the bulge in his pants, while he fumbled with his Smartphone, narrowing down the location of the hospital. After two calls, he'd found out where they had taken her to, Carolina.

Chapter Eighteen

Wendy went to work as soon as she arrived at the hospital. She was on the phone with some of North Carolina's highly political figures, and it hadn't taken long to gather the necessary information to give Danny Dollars.

"I'm here to see Tabitha Fields. They brought her in a little over an hour ago," Cory said to the nurse behind the desk, while Danny Dollars stood off in the near distance.

"Are you any relation?" the while female questioned, knowing he'd say no so she could shoe him away and get back to her crossword puzzle.

"I'm her brother," he screw- faced her.

"Cory, what seems to be the problem?" Wendy asked.

"There's no problem Ms.," she said riposte.

"I'm Tabitha Fields' adoptive mother, this is my son."

Wendy went on to explain that she was a Chief medical official at a local biotech firm and also a leading member of a public work committee. Jeopardizing her esteem status in society, going against all logic, she prayed that she was doing the right thing. Danny Dollars caused a roborant to stir through her. But, these emotions were sure to severe the relationship between her and her husband, who'd climbed the political latter and had been embraced by the movers and shakers who called the shots. Had not her husband's repugnance been so obvious towards Danny Dollars, she would have called him immediately, and the matter would have been settled. But, Wendy didn't understand the magnitude of the situation.

"Mrs., could you please have a seat for a moment? I'll call the doctor so you can speak to him." She gave a half-hearted smile, as she picked up the phone.

The full-figured blond mouthed in a barely audible whisper, and then nodded several times, thus hanging up the phone, and scribbling something on a yellow paper not pad.

A nurse came down the hall and stood behind the work station talking with the blond, as both turned their attention towards the trio. The latter shook her head, as in hating to be the bearer of bad news, and handed the files over to the blond, both taking a seat until the doctor arrived.

An older man who appeared to be in his mid-fifties with salt and pepper hair, dressed in a blinding white shirt and brown slacks, wearing a doctor's jacket walked up to the desk. He peered at some charts and questioned the nurse who pointed towards the three. They were now standing anxiously awaiting word on the condition of Tabitha.

Clearly a foreigner of Asian descent, he strutted over with an outstretched hand and introduced himself.

"The two women were brought in almost two hours ago, neither had identification on them. We only have one survival. Unfortunately, the passenger in the back seat died at the scene."

This was good news to Danny Dollars' ears, although it saddened him to learn Charmaine no longer lived. "What about Tabitha Fields?" Danny Dollars questioned with worried red eyes.

"Considering the severity of the accident, I'd say with proper care, she'll remain in critical but stable condition. She's paralyzed from the waist down and we had to remove her right leg. At this moment, she's going to need all the help she can get."

"Can we see her?" Wendy asked. Danny Dollars was too choked up to respond to the doctor's words.

"Yes, but only for a few minutes, she needs her rest."

"That's understandable. Could you tell us what happened to her? As of now we've been left in the dark, searching for answers."

"From what I've gathered, someone hit the vehicle they were travelling in. The driver of their vehicle must have thought he was at fault, because a witness said he fled from the scene."

"Fled from the scene? Do they have a description?" she fished.

I don't know the reason for the abandonment of the women. This sort of thing happens all the time, could be a warrant, no license… who knows. At this moment, I don't want to speculate. The police only had the height and clothes of the driver who abandoned the car. The other driver, a white, single mother of four, also didn't make it." He eyed Danny Dollars. "Son, you wouldn't happen to be that driver would you? If so you really need to be checked out."

"Doc, I need to know if my girl is alright. I'm not worried about myself," was his only answer.

"I am. If infection sets in I'll be seeing you again, but next time to amputate an arm," he admonished.

Danny Dollars had to listen to reason, although he didn't like it one bit.

Wendy gave him a reassuring look and patted him on the back. Danny Dollars followed the doctor's order. He instructed the nurse to take him to a room. He had put trust in a lot of strangers today, something he definitely wasn't use to.

Cory watched his mentor, observing the way he carried himself in a gentle fashion which was very confusing. This wasn't the *thug life* he saw on the black videos or movie shows, or what he'd seen in the few black friends he had on Bragg St.

"Mom, thanks for helping, Bills. I hope he's not in a lot of trouble, I really like him."

"Yes, he's a good guy who has made a few bad decisions. But I'm going to call Kim while he's seeing the doctor and see what we can do for him." She hugged him, and then pulled out her phone to make the call. Wendy couldn't believe what she was hearing.

Danny Dollars had been implicated in a bloody gun battle in Charlotte. The only evidence was an informant willing to testify that Danny Dollars was part of a criminal ring involved in the deaths of several corrupted officials. The ring leader's wife was said to be a modern day female Capone, who didn't agree to anyone's terms.

"Wendy, maybe you can get him to turn himself in, if not, I'm afraid he'll end up like the rest, meaning in death."

It was true what Danny Dollars had told her. The police had stormed his friend's and cousin's houses killing all occupants, causing a public outcry.

"How can I convince him to do that? It's hard to believe in a corrupt system that's as lawless as the streets."

Kimberly remained silent.

"Mom, I think he'll listen to you. He says you're cool. That says a lot in the streets," Cory added.

With dewy eyes, she responded, "I think he's cool too, son."

Kimberley went on to explain to her that she had to convince him to do the right thing for Tabitha. If he'd risked being locked up to check on her condition, there was enough decency in him to persuade him to do the right thing. Wendy made Kimberley promise to do all she could for Danny Dollars, and she promised, on condition he'd be truthful and help her take down Sulaiman.

Federal Agent Kimberley Canteen walked into the room and her six-five presence was immediately felt. The menacing weapon on her hip along with the look on her expressionless face, warned she had years of experience in target practice and a no nonsense attitude to go along with those years. She flashed her credentials, and his first thought was, *this bitch is a giant*. He wondered why she was chasing bad guys instead of dunking a basketball in the WNBA. There were no formalities, only getting strictly down to business.

"I need to ask you a few questions. But the first will be, do you wish to have an attorney present?" Danny Dollars nodded no. "Okay then, the second question is, do you know why you are being pursued by the police?" Exercising discretion, staring the agent directly in the eye, he repeated the nod.

The brunette met his wandering eyes and ran it down to him, leaving nothing to guess. She explained that she was only doing this because of Wendy and if he lied one time, she'd haul his ass downtown and leave him for the wolves. "As we speak, you're the suspect in a mall shooting last year in Charlotte. They have video footage of you and a distinctive tattoo on your neck of a large big-faced hundred with two capital Ds connected." She pointed to the source.

"You were identified by a witness who's in protective custody as we speak. He's implicated you, your cousin, Antonio 'Tony Killz' Manns, Robert 'Reason' Lee and the ring leader, 'Sulaiman', who officials don't have a last name on, nor do we even know if Sulaiman is his real name or not. As we speak, they're investigating whether or not you and the others suspects have any connections, whatsoever, to the grisly slayings of the agents at the warehouse in Charlotte. Do you wish to confirm you had nothing to do with these killings at the warehouse? Mall security footage already placed you at the scene of the first killings."

The silence was finally broken. He first had to think of his best long term interest. "I'm supposed to go to Japan to meet with Sulaiman for a meeting, that's my man." He shook his head in dismay. "But, no. I had nothing to do with it."

"How long will this meeting last?"

"I don't know. He told me to bring enough clothes for a week," he said, now realizing he may never see the streets again. "If I give you Sulaiman, I want all charges against me dropped."

"If we get a conviction, I'll see what I can do."

"Then this discussion is over. You might as well take me in now if there are no guarantees. This man is invincible. The movies can't even portray a man of his nature. A pure raw killer without a conscious, let's not mention his wife. You people don't realize who you're messing with. These aren't the gangstas of the old days; they're more sophisticated, deadlier, and far more intelligent. They snatch judges, D.A.'s and government officials from their homes. Look at Isis, they have hit lists. No one's afraid of the cops anymore. The street law now is, *you interfere with the operations, and we clap back at you.*"

"I'm well versed in street politics, Mr. Dollars. But the fact remains, you're never going to breathe freedom again, unless you assist me."

"His wife will come after me. As soon as she came home from prison, bodies dropped in New York. Everyone says they were revenge killings."

"Do you want witness protection?" She asked in case he feared for his life.

"No, I want money and a first class ticket to a country of my choice. Those are my terms. Agree, or do what you have to do. The meeting is tomorrow, and if I don't show up, a simple phone call from me will alert him. And once he finds out about the others, you'll never catch him. Time is of the essence and it's running out, Ms. Canteen." Danny Dollars sat back in the chair, the ball was in her hands.

Agent Canteen pulled out her phone and made a call to headquarters. She knew her boss wasn't going to like the deal one bit, but in order to get Sulaiman, he'd just about go along with anything.

It took a lot of convincing and pleading, but within five-minutes a deal was cut, but on one condition only, they wanted Temptation as well….he shook her hand, sealing the deal.

The feds knew this was a major milestone and Tony '357' Rains said nothing about Promises' twin sister who was involved in the kidnapping and murder of Whack's sister. There were a shit-load of unsolved murders, but by the time they finished with the criminal organization of Sulaiman, some of the families would finally have closure.

Danny Dollars couldn't bare it any longer. He held Tabitha's soft hand and knew he had made the correct decision. There was no way he could leave her like this; in fact, he was basically the only family she had left. He couldn't concentrate, so he asked Agent Canteen for a pen and paper. After receiving the requested items, he wrote down the details of a murder he'd committed and left the body dismembered at Sulaiman's Uncle's Farm.

"How's Tabitha holding up?" Agent Canteen asked sincerely, knowing the confession was due to raw emotions. She hated he'd been in a vulnerable state at the moment of questioning, but she had a job to do.

"I would say remarkable, considering the circumstances."

"I spoke with the sheriff while you were with Tabitha. Police have determined the cause of the accident. You weren't at fault." She placed a hand on his slumped shoulder. "The first responder who rushed to the scene was responsible for her being here today. He promptly stopped the bleeding. Wendy and Cory left, they asked that I give you their cell phone numbers." She handed him the digits.

A tall, well-built sheriff knocked on the door. "Come in," Canteen called out, knowing beforehand who the interrupter was. "Danny, this is Sheriff Coleman, he's going to take us to make the identification of the deceased."

"I know this is hard but remain positive. Things could be worst." Coleman's encouraging words were non-effective.

"Could be worse?" Danny repeated, and let out an exasperated sigh. *Is he serious?* He thought to himself.

Coleman said nothing, because in his mind he was only trying to express his concern.

With shaky legs and tear stained eyes, Danny Dollars and Agent Canteen, led by Sheriff Coleman took the elevator to the bottom floor. They descended several stairs to the morgue to identify Charmaine's body.

The cool room caused Canteen's nipples to become erect. Neither of the men meant to stare but couldn't help but notice the buds pushing through the fabric. Both seeing the look on each other's face felt like a piece of shit for their guilty actions.

A woman in her mid-forties with latex blue gloves on was there to greet and escort them to the cooler vault, were the attendant opened it, and there lay the beautiful Charmaine, it was as if she'd been resting peacefully.

Danny Dollars nodded before turning away in shame, there was no mistaken-identity. He gave the sheriff Charmaine's mother's address and phone number. He knew her well, and he'd buy bud from her on the regular since moving from Charlotte.

"Are you okay?" the Sheriff asked sincerely, yet the question came out as always, one of the dumbest.

Danny Dollar thought to himself, *how can someone ask that when they're just days away from burying a loved one?* "Yes," he replied, knowing damn well he was far from okay. "Sometimes, death is a consequence of our own poor choices, and at times, the choices of other's. Are we finished here?"

"Yes. We are. Thanks for the help," Sheriff Coleman said, staying behind to talk with the female who had opened the cooler.

Agent Canteen and Danny Dollar headed back to headquarters, she had to be debriefed and make plans for the trip to Japan.

Chapter Nineteen
Greensboro, N.C.

Temptation cried towards the empyreans, "Why?" She pounded on her lover's nude chest in tears before sliding her nude body from in between the sheets.

The call was from the county jail, explaining that her sister had just committed suicide. They didn't suspect foul play. Temptation needed to get away, drive with the windows down, search for answers, brainstorm- this was devastating. She'd received, yet, another call shortly thereafter of more mind-blowing news as she slipped on her panties and jeans. But, this time the call came from an inmate who said Promise had given her a handwritten letter, and made her swear that should anything happen to her, she'd call the number at the top of the page and read the contents of it then send the letter to her sister.

Temptation was furious, trembling and struggled mentally to come to grips with the lost. *How could her uncle have done such a thing?* She knew he had ill-feelings toward Promise but not to the point where he'd go so far as to set his own niece up. But his actions were unforgivable, and causing Promise to take her life, he had also killed her in the process. In spite of their different path spiritually, they were very much involved in each other's lives.

Out of the numerous obstacles thrown in her path, this had to be by far the worst of the worst ever. She started not to involve Left One, but gave him an honest heads-up. She was a wanted woman and to her, Tony was a dead man. Her lover was on the phone calling a lackey of goons to find Tony and handle the matter, but Temptation knew he was on the run, especially since he hadn't called her on the matter yet. But still, she had to forge ahead with her plans even though she faced tremendous odds against her. She dreaded making the call which had to be made, but it was critical.

"I'm gone, call me in two hours," Left One said as he stuffed two .44 full clips semi-automatics inside his waistband.

Temptation hugged him. "You call me as soon as you get to Charlotte. I want you to snatch a few block huggers up and get anything out of them you can. I doubt anyone knows anything, but leave your mark because when this here is over, I want every figga in the Queen to know Temptation is back." She grabbed his cheeks and squeezed them tightly. "Do whatever's necessary!" She let go getting her point across.

Left One peer into her red, tear stained eyes. There was no way he'd let her down, even if he had to wipe the streets clean.

Temptation walked her lover to the door, kissed him deeply then as if she were losing someone else, walked him to the car to see him off. His men began to pull up, and they were deep.

Promise still should have confronted her. Temptation was mad at her. They were supposed to grow old together, and die together on an Island somewhere with young rich studs. Not only had Tony ruined their lives, he had snitched, which to her was just as unforgivable.

She made a few calls and found out he was put into a witness protection until the case was over. She also found out Danny Dollars made a deal to save the skin on his own black ass, giving up Sulaiman and agreeing to testify. They wanted Zohra, but had nothing concrete. Danny had been taken down to the station, advised of his rights and promptly given a defense attorney shortly thereafter.

"A cheese eating rat," Temptation said as she dialed the number. After about four rings she was about to click off. "I know this bitch is home."

"This better be good, interrupting my private time with my husband," the caller answered and hurled out.

"If it wasn't, I wouldn't be wasting your time or mines…"

"Well, whatever it is, you have two minutes to spit it out."

"We can't talk on the phone, this is confidential. Promise committed suicide in the county jail. My uncle set her up and he's told them about your husband. Now, do you want me to speak to him or what?"

"Temp, this better not be some sick joke of your…," she started to say.

"Listen, you know how I feel about my sister. I'd never wish death upon her, jokingly or otherwise." She choked up.

Zohra said nothing as she allowed Temptation to say as much as possible without incriminating them.

"I'm sorry to hear about Promise. She'll have the best coming home," Zohra said sincerely.

"If you turn on the T.V. you'll see that I'm not pulling your leg. It's been on the Breaking News for at least an hour now."

"Where are you now?" she asked, mouthing to Sulaiman to turn the T.V. to the news. She knew he wanted to see the main event of the MMA fight. She remained silent as Temptation gave her a location, watching her husband's eyes widen in shock.

"Temptation, you weren't thinking. Get out of there, now! They're looking for you, but you said they called you to tell you about Promise. Tony disclosed where you are. Meet me at our old hang-out. Don't answer the phone unless it's me or Sulaiman. Do not trust anyone, for it may have serious repercussions."

"Zohra, who were you on the phone talking to?" Sulaiman questioned.

"Temp, she called to notify you that her uncle gave you up to the cops."

"Her uncle?"

"Come on, let's get on the road. I'll explain the little I know once we're in the car. We're to meet her at Kendrick's place."

Zohra made the call to Kendrick who happened to be dialing her number at the same exact time.

He paced the floor back and forth about to drive Bubbles insane. Bubbles placed her paw over the bridge of her nose and then barked. She knew something was wrong. Annia had been arrested at work, and she'd told them everything about the Rock Hill killings and those responsible. That had only been five minutes ago, and he knew the cops were on their way to his Tobacco Rd. apartment. He'd been alerted by a female co-worker who knew he had pulled out of the wedding at the last minute, crushing Annia's vengeful heart.

Kendrick also gave Zohra some more shocking news. He'd been following up on Temptation ever since she'd told him about the fall out and revealed she was an Aunt. Temptation had secretly withheld a pregnancy from them, having a baby boy by Victorious who was raised by an Aunt at an apartment complex near Ridgewood shopping Center.

"Kendrick, are you absolutely sure?"

"100 percent, I have a copy of the birth certificate and your brother's name is on it." Kendrick paused. "Are you okay, Snowflake?" she side-stepped the question.

"Do you have the document with you?"

"Yes, I have it. The only thing left at my apartment is the furniture. He did leave some clothes so it wouldn't appear he'd fled. Meet me at the last restaurant." Then he disconnected.

"What did he say?" Sulaiman asked.

"I'm an Aunt."

"An aunt, I thought your brother didn't have any kids?"

Hating to even mention her brother since the nightmares had ceased temporarily, she went on to discuss what they may be up against. The four of them would have to put away any differences and organize an effective plan to keep things from further spiraling into total chaos. With an ominous of snitches, one had to be on point at all times.

Kendrick made it to the restaurant first and held down a table for four. The migraine headache was the worst he'd ever had. There was a strong case against them with Annia running her lips, luckily he had back-tracked and cleaned up the area, disposing of the bodies in the Pee Dee River, allowing the man-sized catfish to feast on the remains, which were so generously diced up for them, and scattered throughout a 10 mile stretch.

Temptation arrived next. He had thought she was dead until the incident happened at the mansion in Nyack, NY. She pet Bubbles on the head, never realizing it was a dog friendly establishment.

"This is a pleasant surprise." Kendrick stood up and hugged the lovely Temptation. "I thought you'd died at the mall, word was your body was twitching and your finger still squeezed the trigger."

"Part of that's true, I had been hit. The force of the Ruger P 90 knocked me backwards, but it was a clean exit wound. At the first red light, I bailed from the ambulance and ran through some brush. I blacked-out, and this might sound crazy, but a crack head found me and she used to be nurse. Instead of calling for help, she doctored me up." This was a woman she'd be forever grateful to; the same one Kendrick thought was her Aunt, the one who stayed in a condo taking care of her son.

The two conversed on various topics until the husband and wife came in searching faces until they found the two sorts.

Temptation appeared to be preoccupied on the phone. She had to call Left One. Everyone greeted and waited until she was off the phone so she could concentrate on the meeting.

Temptation ended the call, and it was time to play couthie, even though she knew it would drain her. Shockingly, Zohra hugged her and so did Sulaiman.

What the fuck is going on? She thought to herself. It had to be because of Promise. But she wasn't there for a pity party, she'd come to discuss the contents of the letter and give them what Left One found out. She went on to explain in clear and full detail. Left One had done a heck of a job.

"My boyfriend's sister works in Charlotte at the station. As we know, they do not having anything on us but the statements of Annia and Danny Dollars, they're trying to locate Whack."

"He's in Brazil," Sulaiman said. "He may testify," he added, thinking about their phone exchanges.

"They'll cut him a deal he won't be able to refuse," Zohra said.

"Then we need to find him first and eliminate the others," Sulaiman added. "We have to come out of this clean. It's the only way." His words echoed, *clean...* What he meant was, Whack and the others must die.

"Dee, you're not implicated in any of this and as for speculating, I won't do it, but I do know there's no security camera footage, even though talk on the streets says otherwise.

"I took care of the mall security cameras and the bodies in Rock Hill," Kendrick remarked.

No one could verify all the rumors, but what was fact had to be built upon. Planning for the foreseeable future, they agreed to eradicate all threats. Although they were there on serious business, the four exchanged badinage during a light meal.

Kendrick had picked a great spot for them. Excusing himself from the trio to rid himself of the gas guzzler he'd driven for a more fuel-efficient car, he left the others waiting at the banquette towards the back of the room, away from the crowd. He didn't want to get spotted driving around town, lucky he had a safe house. A cop car drove by slowly and he squatted down as if tying his shoes, waiting for the police to pass by.

He decided to strongly consider turning himself in and work from the inside, but first, he wanted to run it by Zohra to see if she agreed.

Temptation received another call, this time from a neighbor giving more bad news. She already felt as if she'd never recover from the major loss of her sister, now Left One. This definitely ruined her dreams of living happily-ever-after in a large condo overlooking the ocean, and a vacation house out in the Hampton's.

The raid was swift. Police kicked in Temptation's door, entering with guns drawn. Left One slept peacefully in bed and was awakened by the loud thunderous crash. He reached for the gun he'd laid on the nightstand within reach. He'd forgotten the situation, mentally drained by the aggressive style of gathering information. Shots were fired, so much for minimizing civilian casualties, but he didn't get killed. Left One lay critically wounded, yet another foiled attempt. He was rushed to Wake Med, where he lay fighting for his life.

Temptation relayed the news, as Zohra now sat on the phone being drilled by her heated uncle. She smiled when Kendrick returned and ended the call. She explained to Sulaiman that she had to return home and advised him to handle the situation as promptly as possible.

She took Sulaiman's vehicle and drove straight to RDU airport. Her uncle was furious and this wasn't good.

Kendrick got behind the driver's seat and waited as the others came out one-by-one. Sulaiman came out second, took inventory of his surroundings then got into the Lincoln Continental, leaving the back seat for Temptation. She peered around before leaving a gratuity on the table, more than a generous one. She was unaware Left One was undergoing two surgeries amputating a leg and hand.

She was thankful she didn't have to cram into the stolen vehicle. Kendrick made his way through the early morning, congested, metropolitan area, hitting pot holes, crossing a deteriorated bridge, desperately in need of fixing. He drove out to the country after 30 minutes of being stuck in traffic. The ride took an hour and a half.

"Wake up, sleepy head," Kendrick called out to the back.

Sulaiman eyed his Smartphone. The feds were storming his home, and they were on to him, for no one knew of the home but Zohra. He had to think carefully and admonished everyone to make sure safety procedures were followed to the letter, noting that the authorities wanted them more so dead than alive. Lives were at stake and with no clear timetable as to how long they had, the three had to rest up because it was going to be one busy day.

Chapter Twenty

Zohra stepped off the plane only to be greeted by her red-eyed Uncle. At the sight of him, she knew something was definitely wrong.

"Uncle," she whispered, not understanding why.

"Let's take a walk," he said, and then peered around before proceeding.

"What troubles you?"

"For years I've helped groom you to handle yourself properly, but the time has come. You must stop, or you'll ruin us all."

The soft words were a harsh warning. She knew he'd have her killed before he'd rot in a jail cell.

"They had nothing on me or you."

"You can't go around whacking every informant. It brings heat. I'm afraid I can no longer help. You've crossed the limits." He stopped, hands woven behind his back.

"No one knows about your help, not even my husband."

"You don't get it do you? They're using people who'll lie, cheat and steal their way out of a sentence. Guilty themselves, but exchanging testimony for lighter sentences," he stressed. "The feds are chewing my asshole raw. This is bigger than us."

"Nothing or no one is bigger than us. You taught me that." She had to be careful about her critical comments despite her protection from him. For him to want to abandon her, things had to be serious. "You're holding back." She began to feel his trust collapsing.

"You my niece, I always thought you to be the wisest one."

"And, your point?" she asked knowing they only had a slew of accusations for their investigations.

The growing concern had him vexed, such irresponsibility was no excuse. He got a stern grilling by his boss and those above him were working diligently with the feds who had persisted for a little over a year to gather enough Intel on her to take her down, a key component in a dangerous network. Now her husband's troubles came into the fold.

"Either, kill your husband or…"

"Or what?" She stepped closer. Tempers flared. If only he knew her innermost thoughts.

"You've been closely watched since your return."

"How close? How close damnit!" Zohra thundered.

"It's over," he said, and then nodded.

"Out of nowhere federal personnel detained her placing the struggling red-head into custody. The secret operation had taken a year to execute.

Zohra was taken to a van and transported to a facility for questioning. Knowing her status, they had to beef up security. No one was in fear of retribution. All her curfew turned snitches. Witnesses gave statements, told detailed accounts of the number of deaths.

She arrived at the building, staring with contempt in her eyes. She refused to talk to anyone, regardless of the phonebook size statements in front of her. They revealed the inner workings of the cartel. They even knew about the behind-the-scenes men. They proceeded to interrogate her for hours, while corrupt officials with goon mentalities ram shackled her home and businesses. The few loyal who remained with her had destroyed everything with her name stamped on it. She had to stay focused and be prepared.

The same cowards who buckled under harassing phone-calls and threats from rival cartels sided with the enemy out of fear for their lives. Now they were in a jacket in front of her willing to testify before Your Honor. But, she vowed to remain defiant in the ugly face of envy, jealousy and pride. It was time to boldly confront those who deceitfully persecuted her and had her people on the job as well. She wanted snapshots, catching informants entering and exiting unmarked vehicles. She also wanted the police who cordoned the crime scene area, the paid officials who had the police target family members, and those who didn't want to climb aboard and were arrested. She wanted all of them and she wanted them dead! A dead man couldn't point fingers.

The feds also had Suliaman on the list of allegations and they knew he'd killed Black Fats.

She read the words of Danny Dollars: *I watched him cut my friend to pieces. I feared for my life, and had I not went along, I wouldn't be alive today.* Danny Dollars said Kendrick supplied the weapons, as he explained the grimy scene that caused him to turn his head. *Sulaiman* slices necks like sharp cheese then he drops you to the floor and carves you to pieces. He does everyone he kills like that.

"Your witness is softer than drug store cotton." She gave the two agents bar-knuckle insults, she knew her rights and to deny her an attorney was one of them.

Aaron Unique Carter, find 'Whack' and have him and Mica flown in, one of them will testify. Last I heard, they were in Brazil, Sao Parlo. The statements read.

"Have you seen enough Mrs. War?"

Finally speaking after several hours of nothing but gibberish she said, "Yes, I've seen enough. Enough to know you don't have jack-shit on me, statements from convicted felons, on ex-felonies who'll say just about anything to retrieve their precious freedom. As to my husband, he's also clean, and as far as I'm concerned, those dead Agents Clark and Deacon were the bad guys, not us. The moral fabric of honor codes was lost to them, seeking illegal gains."

"You think it's that simple? Any jury will put you away for life," Agent Knox spat.

"We'll, get them ready."

"Your attorney won't be able to save you this time," Agent Ramsey said, pounding his fist on the table.

"Excuse me, Sir. Mrs. War's attorney is here to see her."

"Stupid cops still don't know my name has been changed," she murmured to herself.

"We're not finished with you," Agent Knox said, before storming out trailed by Ramsey.

"Zohra," her attorney hugged her but had a different look in his eyes. "You have a no bond. I need you to get Sulaiman up here to turn himself in. While we're fighting extradition, I can build a solid case for him. So far, there are only a couple of people saying unprovable things related to nothing the papers or media haven't said already. The witnesses haven't been to the warehouse or does he knows where it's located. No one can place him at the mall and as far as the farm killings, the others who can testify are dead, and those still alive wrote statements on your husband's behalf," he said, the files in front of her to observe. "The killing of the families in Rock Hill, your friend Kendrick's girlfriend implicated several people in the murders, only by nicknames.

I can destroy her character in court. She's in the hospital as we speak, took a handful of pills. The judge gave her bond and she went home and tried to take her life. She's on suicide watch as we speak. She also admitted to helping authorities put Kendrick behind bars because he broke her heart."

"Sounds like a scorned lover."

"My point exactly, so, that's pretty much it in a nutshell. Now you on the other hand, it's a little more complicated."

"Meaning?"

He blew out pent up frustration.

"Zohra…"

"Spit it out for Pete's sakes. You know I'm not one to bullshit around." She looked him square in the eyes. "What do they have on me? And can I get a bond?"

"The judge refuses to give you a bond. I've mentioned you had no priors and that you're not a flight risk. I told him about your education and businesses, but he wouldn't budge. They have eye witnesses who're willing to say you committed the crimes, and place you at the scene. They've pleaded to a lesser charge of accessory and for their cooperation most will be given probation, no more than 3 to 5 years, if that. They want you off the streets for good, and they've got you charged with the RICO Act."

"My God, what are you saying?" She covered her mouth.

"Unless you plead guilty to the murders, your only choices are life without the possibility of parole, or death. These… I'm afraid are your options as we stand."

This was a major blow to her.

The agents in the next room had been listening to the supposedly confidential meeting, and wondered her next move, and if she'd disclose it to them.

"Apparently, she's pissed some people off," Knox said.

"Majority of them are dead, seems like they pissed her off," an agent retorted.

"Twenty dollars she throws her husband to the wolves," one said, as he pulled a bill from his pocket.

"Speak for yourself. I'm no wolf," said the no-nonsense agent recording the conversation.

"I'll bet you. She has that look of love. This woman is bull-leather tough."

"I can't count how many cold-hearted killers come in here squalling like a pig."

All nodded their heads.

"Not this one." Agent Young stood firm.

"Well, put up or shut up."

Agent Young slapped a twenty on the desk in front of him and matched anyone else who wanted to wager.

"Tell them to take me back to my cell. I have nothing further to say. I'm no rat, and death means more to me than to live with shame and disgrace." She stood up, shook his hand and told him to focus on Sulaiman. Then, she sat back down. There was nothing more to talk about.

Agent Young smiled, then collected his money.

Zohra was marched upstairs.

※※※

This was Sulaiman's first time in Fayetteville. He didn't realize where he was until after crossing the All American Expressway. Kendrick was glad the bridge wasn't under construction as it had been the last time he'd come to Fayetteville; both North and Southbound lanes had closures. The drive from 401 on Raeford Rd. to Hope Mills Rd. didn't take as long as expected, and the three had settled in, all needing much rest.

Temptation cried herself to sleep. She had stayed on the phone checking up on Left One, conversing with him and his family who were there for him after he'd gotten out of surgery.

His mother was angry, blaming it all on Temptation. When the Detectives came to question Left One, she told them her son had been on the phone several times with Temptation while using her phone. The detectives asked her for the phone, and an hour later they gave it back, went inside and spoke at lengths with Left One, whom they threatened to charge with a slew of charges if he didn't help. He talked her into letting him know of her whereabouts so he could send his sister with some cash so she could go to cross creek mall and purchase clothes and personal hygiene items. Without thinking of betrayal, she gave it to him and told him she'd call back as soon as she received the money. He kept her on the line trying to buy time.

Left One lay his spineless ass in bed, finding it hard to believe, he'd did the unthinkable. No one knew how his heart felt, crushed inside because he truly loved Temptation with all his heart and soul. The enamored thug shed real tears. He kicked everyone out of the room and a scream was heard throughout the building. He had to do something. Maybe once they arrested her and charged her, he could help her with attorney fees as soon as he got better, by taking to the block and going hard in the streets, prosthetic leg and all.

Sulaiman slept a good four hours, straight, before being awakened by his cell phone. He stirred, stretching his tired body, realizing he'd crashed with his clothes on. He reached for his phone which was next to his hat and keys. Peering at the screen, he noticed an unfamiliar number from New York. He answered and the female recording informed him of the collect call from Zohra. Paralyzed with fear, he accepted the call with shaky hands.

"Sulaiman, I'm sorry baby. My Uncle turned me in this time... I'm afraid I won't be able to get out of this one. The snitches are lined up around the block. Everyone has turned. The only ones who kept their traps closed were Reason and Morgan, and they're going to make an example out of them for doing so."

"Slow down, Rd," Sulaiman said, then walked over to the window, opened the curtains, then let the window open to allow the fresh country air inside; it had suddenly become a little stuffier in the room. He inhaled, exhaled, closed his eyes and took in the wild sound of nature and his wife breathing. "Are you okay?" he asked, referring to any physical harm.

"Yes, both Paris and Ayesha were arrested. They separated us. Paris was released and she claimed to only be an employee, which is true. She knows nothing of my legal business or otherwise," she carefully mentioned in case the phones were wired.

"How about Ayesha, she's a caregiver, nanny." He corrected himself.

"She should be released shortly as well. My attorney is representing them both."

"That's great. What about the children?"

"They're with Tracy Dimes. You know the twins love Silhouette."

Whack's daughter was growing fast and she thought Sulaiman was her father, and the twins her sister and brother.

"Does your incarceration have anything to do with me?" He treaded lightly on the subject.

"No, but my attorney has the information I sent him and he's gotten in touch with yours, both agree it's best for you to turn yourself in to the authorities in New York not North Carolina, this will give them the much needed time to delay things while fighting extradition. They only have accusations on you. I don't know who's lying on you but our lawyers are competent enough to get a dismissal of all charges against you," she said. "Don't make them come after you, Sulaiman. I need you up here with me. Promise me that as soon as you put this phone down, you'll be on the road." She pleaded, knowing he should avoid the air.

Zohra wanted to mollify their situation with a heartfelt apology for letting him down, going against his advice. She broke down as he promised, and soon as he hung up he searched for his shoes, closed the window back, tucked the cell phone inside his pocket, put the fitted cap on his head then went to let Kendrick know he was leaving.

Sulaiman hadn't talked to Temptation much, but thought it best she know about Zohra, which made him think about the son she'd failed to tell everyone about.

Temptation stood under the shower head in deep thought. She couldn't sleep, and knowing Left One's sister would be arriving soon, she wanted to go to the mall in downtown Fayetteville.

Kendrick had left a note saying he was going home for a moment to replenish the fridge and to get toiletries. Sulaiman was in the next room and he hadn't said as much as a word to her besides an occasional nod, or a simple *you're right* response. She dried off feeling somewhat reinvigorated, energized, and starving. A knock startled her, breaking her thoughts.

"Yeah," she answered.

"Temp, where's Kendrick?" he asked upset because he'd slept hard and didn't hear the car drive off. He prided himself for being alert during situations like this. "Did he say where he was going?"

Temptation opened the door, her hair was wrapped and only a small towel was around her small waist, but she didn't do much to conceal anything else. She figured he'd seen everything, so it wasn't any use of hiding it.

"He left a note saying he was going out to get food and things, and he'll be back shortly." She eyed him sharply. "Where are you going?"

"I'm going to turn myself in. I think you should do the same. If you choose that route, I'll pay for the best attorney money can buy and we'll beat these charges. They have nothing on us but statements and you leaving from inside an ambulance. No footage from a video."

"Thanks, but no thanks," she said as she put on a shirt she'd found in a closet in the guest room, going braless until her underwear were dry.

"Plus, my boyfriend's sister is on the way to bring me some cash, I need to get myself some clothes and take care of some last minute business."

"Temptation, I don't think you should have given out this location. What if the cops shook him?"

"Stop hating, Sulaiman. You had your chance. He loves me. My first time receiving flowers from a man who loves me...."

"Temp." Sulaiman put his hand on her shoulders. "I'm telling you this because I care for you..."

"No you don't!"

"Please, listen to me. Zohra is locked up in New York. Her crimes are unrelated, and this time, I fear she'll never get out."

"Sulaiman, why are you telling me this?"

"Because, it may just be me and you in the end; only a small moiety of women come out on top in this life."

Is this some cruel moiré? She thought. "Left One isn't like that, and he'll never abandon me, not like the others or you. This is the first time I haven't been hurt by a man."

Sulaiman stood, looking stupefied. How could anyone account for the horrible things done to her in the past? Unfathomable, but it began to register in his mind that he needed to leave or else it might be too late.

"I don't know your boyfriend, but I do know this, should you ever need me, I'm a call away. No one possesses infinite knowledge, if we did, we wouldn't need the man upstairs, but I do know this, I think you're making a big mistake. Here's my number, don't forget it." He rumbled off the digits. "Take this too. I feel you may need it." It saddened him.

Reluctantly, she accepted the gun. "Sulaiman take care. I'm sorry about Dee, you might not believe this but I'll always love her, even though I'm still feeling some type of way about her stealing you from me."

"Temp, you're a mess," Sulaiman said, and then kissed her. "Take care of yourself. Don't forget that number." He repeated it several times until she had it. "Oh, Zohra knows about your son."

She got quiet. "That's why I can't turn myself in," she said, after a moment of thought. "I have to see him first. You do understand?"

"Yes, as much as I hate to admit it." He turned to leave.

"Sulaiman, wait!"

He stopped short of reaching the door.

"Why did you kiss me? You know my feelings for you."

He stood quietly in thought now. "Just know that everything I've said to you, I meant from my heart. I'm here for you if you need me." Again, he kissed her, but this time on the top of her forehead.

With that, he disappeared with an erection, one of those things men just didn't have control over.

Chapter Twenty-One

Temptation's emotions were in a serious tug-of-war. She couldn't get Sulaiman off of her mind and she noticed the struggle he'd had to keep his hands off her body. She'd also noticed the massive hard-on he'd left with. He was the only man she'd cheat on Left One with without a care or regret in the world. She wanted so badly to go with him, but she needed to get this money so her son would be alright. But, somewhere deep in her soul, she felt she'd made the wrong decision. She went to her phone and made sure she'd put his number in.

"Always keep a back-up plan, girl!" she said aloud, placing the gun on the table, as she searched the fridge. *Damn, I see why you went shopping,* she thought to herself. Her stomach sounded off causing her to search the cabinets. "Cereal, that'll do," she said.

Temptation thought back to when life was simpler. Literally, she'd lost it all but she'd be damned if she would remain bound home, a prisoner in someone's house. She did realize she had to slack up on big luxuries, especially since she was on the lam.

At first, Sulaiman's insipid actions were draining, but this morning he'd come alive. *Did he realize that since his wife was now out of the picture, he could now focus on them?* Temptation's mind ran a millions miles per second. *Why did I have to bring up Left One? He might have made love to me on the bathroom sink or floor had I not.*

Temptation couldn't get the dirty thoughts out of her mind. *Temp, your obstinate self may have got you in trouble again.*

After washing the bowl and spoon out, placing the milk jug and cereal back where they belonged, she went into the larger-than-life living room and cut the T.V. on. She took a seat on the sectional, sitting lotus position. The day time soaps were on, but her mind still lingered on playing with Sulaiman's scrotum with her warm lips. Her thoughts turned into dreams as she drifted off only to be awakened 30 minutes later by the sounds of tires kicking rocks down the graveled drive-way.

Suddenly she bolted up and police squad cars were flooding the scene. Fear came into fruition; her fist initial thought was either Kendrick or Sulaiman had set her up. *Had the web of deception started when Sulaiman pretended to care? Had it all just been smoke and mirrors, lies and deceit?*

The view was clear until something was tossed into the window, then an unpleasant odor and smoke engulfed the room. She jumped up and reached for the gun with all-out war on her mind. If she couldn't kill those directly responsible, she'd get those who sort to bring her to justice by all means.

She had to move quickly before she found herself surrounded by agents from all side. She grabbed the gun, and burst out of the back door as they ran from their cars, prompting the deputies and agents to open fire. Temptation ran for dear life, a track star didn't have anything on her.

Running through brambly bushes, prickly leaves, scratching her skin pushing on, as dogs barked closing in on her trail. Thanks to her daily workouts, she wasn't winded. She had to radically change her strategy. There was no possible way to out run the K-9. From the sound of the barking, there was two of them, three at the most. She hid behind a tree, the barky property had been abandoned, seemed like for years. As soon as the first dog jumped, with perfect timing the knife she pulled from her jeans back pocket punctured the German Sheppard's lung; she twisted then dropped the dog, but not before taking a few bites of the arm of the second brown Sheppard who had his neck sliced.

"I just added two charges to a laundry list," she murmured, unconcerned about any future reprisal, knowing her actions would bring forth an angry reaction.

All that secret training with Zohra back in the days had paid off. Now, she had to switch up her route and throw them off. If she headed south, keeping close to the tree line, maybe she could carjack some unfortunate victim using her feminine lure. Her destination was back to Raleigh, and determined as ever, she wasn't going to stop until she got there.

Her phone rang and she started to answer it, but decided to clear more distance, so with the phone on vibrate she continued on.

Sulaiman sighed, "Why aren't you answering, Temp?" he said, as he stood at the store's pay phone.

Several times he had to duck into the woods because of the cop cars and black SUV's that shot past him. He realized how stupid the hustlers were emboldening the cops to pull them over because of their baggy pants sagging, fitted caps and gold chains, bumping loud music. Any moment a cop could be yelling *"assume the position asshole "or" you know the drill"* making them soil the brand new gear, but today they were the least thought about. He heard one guy asking another if he had that Miami on him, *'round here, they do random searches,"* he said.

Sulaiman called a cab who confirmed he'd be there shortly. While waiting, he eyed Kendrick who had stopped at the red light, not wanting to draw too much attention. Swiftly he walked to the edge of the street and flagged him down, snatching Kendrick's attention.

Kendrick whipped the vehicle into the store's parking lot but Sulaiman directed the car towards the back, causing the nosey ass dealers to think he was stealing sells. One of the dudes called out to another and they all followed him behind the store.

"My nigga, I know you ain't gonna disrespect us like that."

"Bruh, I'm just catchin' a ride with my man. No harm in that is it?"

"Oh, you one of those New York cats?"

"Like I said, I'm keepin' it movin'."

"Yeah, you better push it."

Kendrick had had enough. He got out of the car and without warning he went at the three with lightning speed. The three didn't have a chance.

"I see you've been practicing."

"Someone has to teach idiots a lesson and I have a thing about sparing the rod." He laughed. "Where's Temp, if you're here, she has to be alone."

"I tried my best to get her to come with me, but she's stubborn. I tried to call her but she's not answering her phone. I saw three cruisers headed your way."

"Where were you headed?" The questions continued to pour forth. Realizing how things looked from Kendrick's perspective, Sualiman hadn't even called him.

Sualiman explained everything. "Damn, she must think we set her up.

"We? Bruh, *we*!" Kendrick said, raking his fingers through his hair.

"Fuck!" Sulaiman swore, unable to tame his last profanity.

"Get in, no need for us to get hauled off because of these clowns." He was furious with himself for leaving.

"She won't answer the phone. It's a good possibility she's in custody."

"Let's hope she saw them coming and fled, unable to answer. I had the place specially built where I can see everything before it comes. Shit!" Kendrick noticed four squad cars speeding past them.

"Pull over into that pathway over there. Get a move on it before the three amigos wake up and jot this tag down."

The men drove about twenty yards and eased down the dirt path backwards.

"Let's wait awhile to see if they pass by with her. If they've apprehended her, we'll drive to New York." Sulaiman went on to explain the conversation he'd had earlier with Zohra.

The two waited for what seemed like forever. More cars passed by, and a helicopter could be seen in the far distance. They were sure she was on the run or searching for them.

Sulaiman got out of the car to go answer the office of nature. The long held urine came out in a gush, the relief caused him to close his eyes and he liquefied the tree trunk. His eyes shot wide open at the feel of cold steel.

"Give me one reason why I shouldn't blow your fuckin' brains out over this field," the distinctive female voice threatened.

Sulaiman said nothing as he shook his dick dry, stuffed it back inside his boxers then answered, "Because, we're sitting out here waiting on you to answer the damn phone. Now, put that shit up so we can get the hell out of here. Soon they'll search everything in a 10 mile radius."

Temptation dropped the gun down from his temple, tucked in behind her, then climbed into the back seat. "I apologize if I was too damn busy to answer the phone, and I was a little preoccupied." She huffed.

Kendrick peered to the back from the mirror. "You look like shit."

"You alright?" Sulaiman asked as Kendrick pulled off slowly. He noticed the cuts and bruises to her face and arms. The clothing she wore was damn near ripped to shreds, a $1300.00 Polo shirt gone to waste. "Toss that phone of yours as soon as we hit this bridge coming up. There's a GPS on it and every time you use it, they can locate you. I warned you about your lover. He set you up, weak ass dudes always do that," he said, and then turned around in disgust, not allowing her to answer the original question.

"Let me out downtown. I'm not going anywhere until he's dead," she spat venomously.

"We don't have time for that, Temp. Let it go, it is what it is."

"Hell no! Either you let me out or I'll tuck and roll out this bitch." She cried war. "It doesn't make a difference to me. He has to die. I'm going to the hospital to get his ass. Plus, I told his sister what kind of car we were driving so she would know the house when she saw it."

"Don't worry. What's done is done. We'll just have to ditch it. No biggie. But she's right, dude has to die," Sulaiman said, eyeing Temptation who slung the phone into the river. "But I'm going with you, and then we all taking our asses to New York."

"What about transportation?"

"Get to Charlotte and once there we'll get my cousin Robin to give us a car. I left her with several of my brother's cars." He pulled out the phone, called her and made sure she had money and the Audi 54 ready for them once they'd arrive.

Sulaiman was glad to hear Robin's voice, at one time, he thought Whack had raped and killed her but he freed her and his mother, Robin's mother Helen wasn't so lucky.

In no time, Kendrick had them back in Raleigh. He stayed out in the country with his grandmother until night fall, listening to her pray over them all, pleading for them to turn themselves in and let Jesus take care of it all. Kendrick went into the barn and came out with a black duffle bag stack with $375,000.00 in cash. When he returned, his grandfather was pulling up in his beat-up Ford.

"Son, you've been on the news. You're a wanted man. Now, those cops done came down here asking about you and that lawless gong of killers you're with, and you have the balls to bring that criminal activity to your family's home?"

"Pops, it's not what you think. We're going to turn ourselves in but first we need money to hire good representation. Otherwise, they're going to do whatever they have to do to convict us even if they have to lie under oath."

"So, you'll have me to believe law abiding cops and citizens out of the blue, just want to bring false charges against you."

"Dad, I don't have time to argue or explain, but trust me."

"Boy, I didn't raise you like this. You served your country and now look at you. Rogue just like them damn ISIS terrorist. Well, I'm not going to have it. Not in my house or country. I pay taxes, served my country and go to church," Kenneth said, going to get his shot gun from the back of his F-150.

Kendrick had to act fast, with quick thinking, he put his father in a sleeper hold and within a few seconds, the big fellow was out. This should last until they got away from the area but soon as he awakened, authorities were sure to be notified.

Kendrick dashed to the truck, tossed the duffle bag inside to car and went inside to get Sualiman and Temptation who'd been forced to eat a delicious country home cooked meal. Sulaiman had never eaten fried turkey before but it was so mouth-watering he swore it wouldn't be his last.

"Grandma, Pops is in the truck sleeping. He must be bone weary tired, passed out while I was talking to him. I guess work and being worried about me has taken a toll on him. Anyway, don't disturb him, give him about 30 mins. Me and Sulaiman are going to put him in bed, check up on him in about 30 minutes, maybe an hour so he can eat and wash up."

"Oh, heavens, he's been working hard all day in that hot sun. He won't stay out that tractor. I'll reckon I'll let him rest. It's the only way it seems like he's going to get it."

"Come on, Sulaiman. Help me get the old man inside."

Sulaiman excused himself from the table and thanked Ms. Mary and joined Kendrick.

Once outside he went on to explain. "Sulaiman, I had to put him to sleep. He was going for the shotgun.

Let's get the hell out of here before he wakes up ranting and raving."

The men both struggled with the 6'4" 305 pound of a man with 55 lbs. of it his stomach, laboriously they managed to get him inside and Mary slipped him out of his muddy work boots.

Sulaiman and Temptation were waiting outside in the car, while Kendrick explained to his grandmother what had really happened to her son. She was bound to find out anyway. He promised her that he'd turn himself in to prove his innocence.

Ms. Mary walked him to the car where the two thanked her once again. She handed all three plates to take with them. Kendrick had never lied to her before and she trusted him to do the right thing. He gave her Zohra's lawyer's number and told her to call and confirm things in the morning, and she planned to do.

Chapter Twenty-Two

Federal Agents captured Whack in his Brazil condo, threatening to turn him over to the Brazilian government officials if he didn't comply to their demands by fully cooperating with them and returning to the States to testify against the most wanted fugitive, Sulaiman, a Central Key figure in the murders of several agents and detectives and numerous murders, a menace to society.

Whack sat on the sofa as if he was entertaining guest. He didn't seem fazed by them being there, especially with gunmen on roofs to take them out should he be taken into custody and give the signal.

The four agents didn't cut any corners or hold punches, and told him what was expected of him.

He gave Agent Canteen direct contact, eyeing her loving cleavage. He noticed the four didn't have weapons or badges. All were dressed casually in jeans or slacks. Her Ralph Lauren eyewear, Gucci turtleneck and Louis Vuitton made him want to bone her something badly.

"Mr. Carter or do you prefer Whack?" she said, her long legs turning him on. He'd always had the hots for a woman his height, it was rare.

"I prefer Whack if this is formal, but if it's business, Mr. Carter."

"This is both, Mr. Carter," she said, eyeing the beauty of the condo.

"Well, have a seat. This looks like it's going to take a while."

"We'll get straight down to business," Agent Ford added, as Whack motioned for everyone to sit.

Whack tried to pretend everything was copacetic but he sensed more than just wanting him to do the right thing and turn himself over; they feared Sulaiman as much as he did, especially since he'd done gone off and married into the mob, defying the rules.

"Seems like you've established quite a life here for yourself," Agent English spoke, with a hint of jealousy.

"You being on the run, one would think it impossible to enjoy the lavish life."

Agent Evans added, "Hiding in plain sight. I've done my homework and you've stole millions in petty scams."

"Life requires personal sacrifices," Whack said nonchalantly.

"Sacrifices Mica wasn't willing to abide by Mr. Carter?" Agent Canteen questioned.

"If you must know, Mica wanted to control me. I'm uncontrollable. Now, Lelia, right there, she's very understanding." The Brazilian bombshell smiled, looking like she dripped from morning honey dew. "She knows her position, very disciplined and not to add she's a freak like me, very high natured." He stared Canteen in the eyes.

The three Agents' minds wandered to those places men wish to go to with a woman of such magnitude.

"Canteen, Ms. that is. I know you've also done your homework, so you know where I'm coming from. I'm going to put it like this, plain and simple. You don't have anything on me, nor do I very seriously doubt that you have anything on Sulaiman. Either I or Sulaiman was at that mall…"

"What about the warehouse?" Agent English thundered losing his cool. He snarled then swore, "Fuck this shit! I don't have to put up with your foolishness!"

"We can haul your ass off right now!" Ford stood up using old school tactics.

"Do you really think those killers on the roof will allow you to do so?"

Lelia slid the pump sawed-off shotgun from the couch and trained it on Agent English's gut.

"Are you fuckin' insane?" he asked, standing white-knuckles scared.

"I'm not, but she might be if you continue to raise your voices in my home disrespectfully."

Canteen stepped in, "Agents, please go to the car. I wish to talk to Mr. Carter Alone," she stated, trying to defuse the tension in the air.

"No way!" Ford protested.

"If he or his robot does anything to you, I'll never live with myself."

The cocking of the shotgun let him know Lelia was just about fed up with the insults.

"Had your lives been in danger, you wouldn't be standing here. Mica may have issues with me, but she has eyes on her at all times. I smelled you miles away, actually, as soon as you flew in I was notified. By that same government you think you're going to turn me into. I do my homework as well, that's why you're in plain clothes. They refuse to let you take me back. I'm too valuable to them." He removed his cell phone and tossed it to Agent Canteen. "Call him! Who, Agent Canteen? Roger's."

This was the same guy who refused to let them take him in. She dialed the number on the card she'd pulled from her front pocket. Confidently assertive that he couldn't be serious, but on the first ring, Roger's answered. The two spoke, she became quiet, then handed the phone to Whack. The blaze had been extinguished quickly before it got out of hand.

Agent Canteen wanted to speak to him in private, but her fellow colleagues wouldn't allow it. She knew Whack wasn't going to harm her. In fact, she wished that she'd came alone, the agents made matters worse. They were instructed to let her handle everything and only assist in her lead, but chances were slim of accomplishing anything of value.

Mica claimed to be a victim herself. She killed Whack's sister by mistake. She'd lost her family as well and never forgot Tony Killz name being called out. She gave Agents full details of everything leading up until the mall shooting, but couldn't place Sulaiman at any of the crime scenes. For her cooperation, no criminal charges would be filed, even though she wouldn't go to court and testify. Mica struggled financially, and she being under surveillance didn't know they were aware of her sleeping with four different men the night before, blind to the fact that she was saving enough cash to purchase a K&I, a room for the weekend, and a hot meal. The car she did have, had to be traded in for substantially less money than paid for, the cash had went a little quicker than expected.

Mica had a rough time. At first, the streetwalkers were weary of her American status. The money flocked to her. Had she known the ropes, she could have been a high class whore, but she managed to avoid conflict. Most became friendly, wanting to know about the great American. Some sort of international conflict happened between her and Whack, but neither disclosed their issues.

"Mr. Carter, if you decide to change your mind and wish to speak to me, here's my number," Agent Canteen said as she handed him a while business card. "Please don't hesitate to use it."

"Ms. Canteen, if you decide to change your mind and wish to speak to me, here's my number," Whack said, then groped his thick dick in his hand. "Please, don't hesitate to use it, I'll be waiting." He laughed wickedly as the other Agents told her to come on.

She smiled at his antic; he had managed to get under the men's protective skin.

"You have a good day, Mr. Carter."

"Ms. Canteen, my door is always open to you. But, next time leave those stiff cocks. I promise you, you'll never want to leave me." This time, there wasn't any laughter.

"I like her," commented Lelia.

"She'll be back. I guarantee you," Whack said as Agent Canteen closed the door, thinking about the possibilities.

He pulled out his phone and dialed a number he knew by heart, one he dialed once a month. "You busy?" He spoke into the receiver as Lelia went to the window to watch the Agents leave. She noted they'd seen the shooters on the roof tops and made haste to depart.

"Naw, just getting in to New York from Raleigh, sorry I missed your call, something came up," Sulaiman said.

"Four agents just left my condo asking about you, wanting me to rat your ass out. They're still alive, but give me the call and I'll make it do what it do."

"Naw, all's good, we've taken care of most of the witnesses and there's no tape of either of us."

"How's my daughter? Growing fast, looking like a little goddess."

Thanks to Zohra, she'd put Whack in a position with her overseas connections to live prosperous, as long as he remained quiet and ran her operations with her Brazilian mafia friends. Once a month Whack would Skype with his daughter; Sulaiman offered to fly her out, but Whack wanted to wait until she was old enough to go to school. Mica was furious with him for kissing and making up with the enemy, but he'd tired of petty hustling and living in roach infested shacks and eating the same old shit damn near every day. Sulaiman found him and gave him a lifeline with a deal he couldn't refuse.

Sulaiman went on to explain his current situation. He wanted Whack to consider returning to the States. Sulaiman wanted Whack to take over Zohra's operations while she battled her court case, and what better person to do it than Whack, and with an iron-hand. He knew this would piss a lot off but order needed to be restored, especially while Sulaiman waged a war on those who had set his wife up.

Available now from
Lavish Life 88 Entertainment Inc.

"Tailor Made Candy Part 1" - by Erskine Harden

"Sabotage to Success"- by Erskine Harden

"The Final Round"- by Darnell Jacobs

"The Upheaval in Rome" – by DonQuell Speller

"A Storm Is Brewing"- by DonQuell Speller *(Storm Series)*

"Cognitive Behaviors of Lola Lohan" by DonQuell Speller

"Why Do You Let Him?"-by DonQuell Speller

"Urban Millionaires"- by Willie Smith

"Cheaters Never Win" – by Dwight Jordan

"Poetry in Plain Sight"- by Lavinia Jackson

"Mind Blowing Clique"- by Willie Smith

"Live by the Gun Die by the Gun"- Keith Robinson

The Anatomy of Hip Hop by Anthony Boone & Erskin Harden

"The Upheaval in Rome II: Revenge of the Eternal City" DonQuell Speller

Summer 2015 Releases

"Crackhead Larry" -by Anthony Booth

"*Frost Bitten*" –by Tony Booth

"The Storm Series: Lynette" -by DonQuell Speller

"The Storm Series: Rage of Lynette" by DonQuell Speller

"The Storm Series: Mahaila" -by DonQuell Speller

"The Storm Series: Mahaila's Destructions" -by DonQuell Speller

"*Tailor Made Candy II* "- by Erskine Harden

"Inside out the Prison Game" -by Tony Booth

"Psychological Study of Delilah Star Cognitive Behavior II" -by DonQuell Speller

Final Round: The Revenge -by Darnell Jacobs

Title	Quantity	Price	Total
Lavish Life 88 Entertainment, Inc. Order Form			
The Anatomy of Hip Hop		$15.00	
Tailor Made Candy Part I		$15.00	
Live by the Gun Die By the Gun		$15.00	
Cheaters Never Win		$15.00	
Poetry in Plain Sight		$15.00	
Urban Millionaires		$15.00	
Mind Blowing Clique		$15.00	
The Final Round		$15.00	
Upheaval In Rome I		$15.00	
The Physiological Study of Delilah Star		$15.00	
Upheaval In Rome II		15.00	
I, Dee Claire War I		$15.00	
A Storm is Brewing		$15.00	

Mail Order Form along with payment to:

Lavish Life Entertainment 88, Inc.
P.O. Box 481367
Charlotte, NC 28269
(908) 552-6687

Email:
info@lavishlife88.com
Website
www.lavishlife88.com

Milton Keynes UK
Ingram Content Group UK Ltd.
UKHW040139170224
437973UK00001B/128